ARABIAN NIGHTS
Storybook

ARABIAN NIGHTS Storybook

Retold by Anoif Maharg

TREASURE PRESS

First published in Great Britain by Ward Lock Ltd
as *Arabian Nights*

This edition published by Treasure Press
59 Grosvenor Street
London W1

ISBN 0 907407 50 1

Printed in Czechoslovakia
50453

INTRODUCTION

Long ago, the Sultan Schahriar, believing all women to be faithless, swore to take a new wife every night and have her put to death the following morning.

His Grand Vizier's beautiful daughter, Scheherazade, volunteering to become his next wife, avoided execution by telling a wonderful story each night, until after a thousand and one nights, Schahriar reprieved her.

This is the simple framework of *Alf Layla wa Layla* —"A Thousand Nights and a Night"—the popular collection of Oriental tales known in English as *The Arabian Nights Entertainment*, from which the delightful stories in this book are taken.

Although the origin of the tales is unknown, they have certainly been altered and added to over the centuries and have probably existed in much their present form since being arranged together by some Egyptian story-teller in the 15th century.

Since they were translated from Arabic into French in 1704, these stories have become as much-loved by people in the West as the traditional folk-tales of Europe.

CONTENTS

Aladdin and the Magic Lamp

Aladdin and the magic lamp

In Persia there once lived a tailor named Mustapha. He was so poor that he could hardly support his wife and his son Aladdin. Aladdin was always mischievous and disobedient, and as soon as his father's back was turned he would run off to play in the fields instead of helping him in his shop.

When Aladdin was fifteen his poor father died, and as Aladdin had never learned to be a tailor, the shop had to be sold. Each day he grew more idle and lazy.

One morning when he was playing in the street, a stranger came up and spoke to him. Unknown to Aladdin this man was a magician in disguise, and had come all the way from Africa to find out about Aladdin and his family.

"Are you Mustapha the tailor's son?" he asked.

"Yes I am," replied Aladdin, "but Father died a long time ago."

On hearing this the stranger grew so excited that he suddenly embraced Aladdin.

"Alas," he cried, tears streaming down his face. "This is indeed sad news, for your father was my dear brother. I am your uncle."

He then asked where Aladdin's mother lived, and giving him a gold coin said:

"Go, Aladdin, and give your

Aladdin talks to the magician who tells him he is his father's long-lost brother from Africa.

The magician threw a liquid onto the fire which Aladdin had made and purple smoke curled into the air.

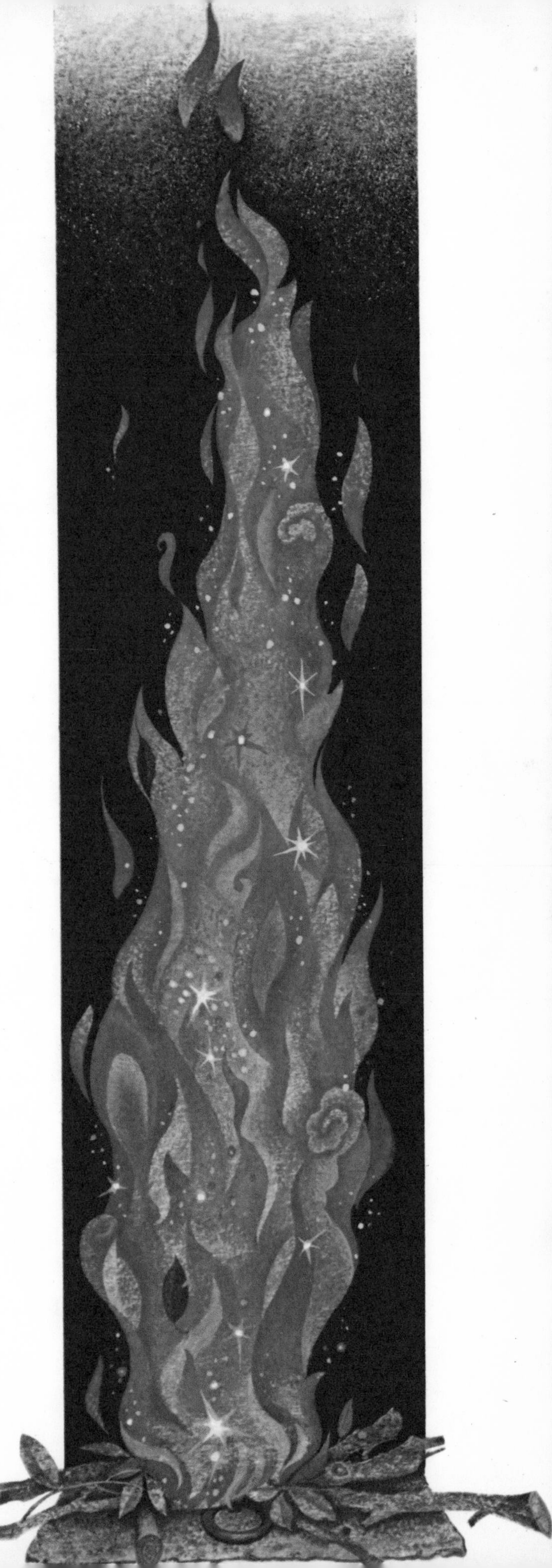

mother my respects. Tell her I shall come and dine with her tomorrow. She can buy food and drink with this money."

"But Aladdin," said his mother in surprise, when he arrived home and told her what had happened. "Your father had no brother, and therefore you cannot have an uncle. How very strange!"

When the magician arrived the next evening he introduced himself to Aladdin's mother, and in order to avoid suspicion he cleverly explained that they had never met before because he had only just returned to Persia after being away for forty years.

"What does Aladdin do for a living?" he asked.

"Nothing," replied Aladdin's mother sadly. "He is very lazy and I can hardly earn enough money for us to live on"—and she burst into tears.

"But I have a plan," the stranger said to Aladdin. "You must try to help your mother. I shall buy you a shop and merchandise, then you will never be poor again. Tomorrow you and I will look for a place."

The magician ordered Aladdin to go into the cave and bring back to him the old oil lamp.

Aladdin's mother was so grateful that this offer convinced her he was indeed Aladdin's true uncle. She never suspected his evil plan, and agreed to the idea at once.

So they both set off next day, and soon the city was far behind them.

"Uncle, why have we left the city?" asked Aladdin, very puzzled, as they approached the hills.

"Watch, nephew!" replied the magician, who was gathering some twigs and starting a fire.

Then he threw a liquid onto the flames and a purple smoke rose into the air. Suddenly the ground beneath them began to shake and Aladdin was struck with terror. A few minutes later the ground started to crack and in place of the fire appeared a square stone trapdoor with an iron ring in the centre. Aladdin was so frightened that he tried to run away, but the magician grabbed his arm.

"Do not be afraid, you silly boy," he shouted, "just obey everything I say. Under this trapdoor are some stone steps which lead to a huge cave filled with the greatest treasure you have ever seen. You can have it all if you just listen!"

"Tell me what I must do, Uncle," answered Aladdin, still shaking with fear.

“Good! Come here!” shouted the magician, “and listen to me carefully. I am too fat to go down myself, so you must go. When you reach the bottom of the steps you will see three caves on your right full of gold and silver. Do not stop in the first two, for I want you to go straight to the third one. In it you will see an old lamp. This is what I want. Hold the lamp carefully and bring it to me at once. The rest of the treasure is yours!”

Thrilled with the offer of such

Aladdin picked up the lamp and called to the magician.

wealth in return for just looking out an old lamp, Aladdin's fear turned into excitement. The magician gave him a magic ring to guard him from any danger, and Aladdin jumped into the opening in the ground, and went down the steps. He found the entrance to the third cave and went inside.

The cave was full of jars of precious stones which sparkled in the dim light. There were diamonds, pearls, sapphires and emeralds everywhere. Aladdin quickly stuffed as many as he could into his sash and found the lamp. Then he made his way back to the entrance of the cave where the magician was eagerly waiting.

"Have you got the lamp?" called the magician.

"Yes," replied Aladdin, "but it's only a dirty old oil lamp, and there's piles of precious stones scattered all over the floor of the cave. Shall I collect some?"

"Give me the lamp first," snapped the magician.

"But it will only take me a minute," said Aladdin.

"Come here at once," screamed the magician.

"Give me your hand to help me up, Uncle," shouted Aladdin.

"First pass me the lamp!" replied the magician, greedily.

"Help me first, Uncle, and then I shall give you it."

Although the magician insisted on getting the lamp first of all, Aladdin refused to hand it over. At this, the magician flew into such a violent rage that he muttered a spell, and the entrance to the cave suddenly closed. Aladdin was a prisoner inside!

Aladdin, of course, had no idea that this man was not his uncle. The magician had discovered by magic that there was a wonderful lamp in a cave somewhere in the middle of Persia. It was a magic lamp, and whoever was lucky enough to own it, would be the most powerful person in the world. The magician would not rest until it was his, but how could he get it?

This was the very reason why he had come all the way from Africa and befriended Aladdin. Aladdin had seemed such a simple and rather stupid boy, who was ideal for the task of going into the cave and finding the lamp. The magician had planned to kill Aladdin when he had given him the lamp, for he wanted no one to know that he possessed it. He had been in such a hurry to obtain the lamp that his own temper had now ruined his only chance of owning it. The precious lamp and all its magic power that he had wanted, were still inside the cave. Furious, he decided that there was nothing he could do but return to Africa immediately, so later that very day, the unhappy magician left to journey back to his native land.

Feeling very frightened, Aladdin called out to the magician many times, promising to give him the lamp, but his cries were useless, and nothing happened. The only thing to do seemed to be to wait and die. He sat down miserably on the cold steps of the cave, thinking all was lost. He would never see the outside world or his dear mother again, he thought.

However, Aladdin was soon to have a surprise. He knew nothing of the magical powers in the lamp or the ring that the magician had given him.

For two days Aladdin wept at

Aladdin's mother was startled by the fierce green Genie.

his fate. Thinking that he would certainly die, he lifted his hands in prayer, and accidentally rubbed the ring which he was wearing on his left hand. Immediately an enormous fierce Genie rose up in a cloud of smoke in front of him! Aladdin could not believe what he saw.

"I am the slave of the ring and ready to obey you! What do you command, oh Master?" asked the Genie. Normally, Aladdin would have been speechless with terror, but he was so afraid of dying in the cave that he immediately answered:

"Oh please, take me out of here!"

The next thing he knew, he was standing outside the rock, exactly where the magician had first brought him. He was so relieved, that he immediately set off home with the lamp, even though he felt so weak after his stay inside the cave.

His mother was overjoyed to see him, for she had thought him lost. When Aladdin showed her the lamp and the jewels, and told her his story, she was furious with the evil magician. As they were so poor she decided to sell the old lamp that Aladdin had brought back the next day, to buy food. Because it was covered with dust and oil, she decided to clean it.

As soon as she started to rub the lamp, a fierce green Genie rose up in front of her, just like the one in the cave.

"What is your command?" the Genie shouted. "I am the slave of the lamp!"

Aladdin's mother was so startled that she fainted and fell to the floor.

"Bring us some food," Aladdin shouted, for he was not afraid, this second time.

Immediately, the Genie brought him twelve magnificent silver dishes piled high with delicious meats, bottles of rare wines and silver plates and cups. Then he disappeared.

When she had recovered, Aladdin's mother was astonished to see such expensive food on the table.

"But Aladdin," she stammered, "what miracle is this?"

"Don't be afraid, mother," said Aladdin.

"But it's so frightening," cried the old woman.

"It's only the slave of the lamp," replied Aladdin. "My magic ring also has a Genie. As I told you, it was the Genie of the ring that got me out of the cave."

"You're sure it won't harm us?" she stammered.

"No, no, mother," Aladdin said. "Don't be afraid."

Whilst they ate the delicious food, Aladdin explained to her what had

No one was allowed to look upon the Princess.

happened, and told her not to be afraid, but be glad at their good fortune.

But Aladdin's mother was afraid of the magical power of the ring and the lamp, and begged Aladdin to get rid of them, but he refused.

"With your permission, mother," he answered, "I should like to keep them both. They can be of great value to us, if we use them sensibly. But take care not to let our neighbours know of our good luck."

As there was some truth in what he said, she agreed. The next day, Aladdin went to sell the fine silver plates the Genie had brought them, and soon the lamp had made Aladdin and his mother very wealthy. Gradually, Aladdin met the rich people in the city, and as he now wore beautiful, expensive clothes, they were eager to make friends with such a prosperous young man.

One day when Aladdin had gone out, he heard the town crier ordering everyone to return home and stay indoors as the Sultan's daughter, the Princess, was passing through the streets. As no one was allowed to look upon the Princess, by law, Aladdin was most curious to see her, and hid around a corner. Soon she appeared, carried through the streets by her slaves. It was the custom for women to wear a veil in that country and when she was very close to Aladdin she happened to lift the veil from her face. Aladdin then saw the most beautiful girl he had ever set eyes upon, and he immediately fell madly in love with her.

He rushed home excitedly to tell his mother.

"Mother! I have fallen so deeply in love with the Princess that I shall not be happy until I marry her! You must go and seek permission from the Sultan at once!"

"Aladdin!" said his mother, laughing in astonishment, "have you gone mad? How could you, a tailor's son, marry the daughter of our Sultan? Even if I did go, he would think I was stupid. Besides, no one can ask the Sultan a favour without offering him a priceless gift. What could you offer him?"

"But I have enough wealth to keep the Princess in a fine palace," Aladdin said. "She can have all the jewels and silks she desires."

"You're only the son of a poor tailor," replied his mother. "What chance have you to marry the Sultan's daughter when all the princes of Persia are seeking her hand? Anyway, there's still the question of a priceless gift. Without one there's no point in my going to the palace."

"Have you forgotten the magnificent jewels I found in the cave, mother? The Sultan will jump with joy at the sight of them!"

Aladdin was so determined, that his mother finally agreed. The next day, having arranged the most beautiful jewels in a gold dish for the Sultan, she left for the palace. But so many people wanted to see the Sultan, that she returned home disappointed. However, on her fourth visit, the Sultan asked to see her, for he had noticed her in the crowd every day and wondered what she carried. Kneeling before him, she offered him the jewels and told him of Aladdin's love for his daughter, and his desire to marry her. The Sultan was delighted with Aladdin's gift. He had never seen such large, dazzling jewels in his life, and was speechless with amazement.

"Is not a man who sends such fine riches worthy of my daughter?" he cried joyfully to the Grand Vizier.

Now the selfish Grand Vizier wanted his own son to marry the Princess, so he persuaded the Sultan to delay the wedding for three months.

"Go home, good woman," the Sultan replied. "I agree to the marriage in three month's time."

When Aladdin heard the good news from his mother he thought himself the happiest man alive! But when three months had

Aladdin's mother presented the Sultan with the beautiful jewels.

Aladdin goes to the Sultan's palace.

almost passed, he learned that the Grand Vizier's son was going to marry the Princess, so he sent his mother back to the Sultan to remind him of his promise. As the Sultan did not want Aladdin to marry his daughter, he had forgotten all about him, and was surprised to see his mother. The only way he could prevent the marriage was to ask Aladdin for so much wealth in return for his daughter that he would not have enough.

"Tell your son he must send me forty large gold basins full of priceless jewels, carried by eighty black and white slaves," was the Sultan's request.

When Aladdin heard this, he quickly rubbed the lamp, and soon, with the Genie's help, the dazzling procession was approaching the Sultan's palace through the astonished crowds. The Sultan wept with joy at the sight of such great wealth and the speed with which Aladdin had sent it, and immediately agreed to the marriage. When he saw Aladdin and his mother approaching, he ran from the palace to embrace them both. As Aladdin was far richer than the Grand Vizier's son, the Sultan was now most anxious for him to marry his daughter.

"Oh mighty Lord," begged Aladdin, "please allow me to build a palace before the wedding, to match your daughter's beauty."

Thrilled to have such a generous son-in-law, the Sultan told Aladdin to put it beside his own one, and only a day later the Genie had constructed one of the most magnificent palaces the Sultan had ever seen!

Invited to look inside, the Sultan's pleasure grew and grew until he was

The Sultan agrees to the marriage of his beautiful daughter to Aladdin.

speechless with admiration.

"Aladdin, nowhere have I seen anything as beautiful as this. It is one of the wonders of the world. You are indeed worthy of my daughter's hand."

So, in spite of the Grand Vizier's protests—for he had grown extremely jealous of Aladdin's success—the happy couple were married next day. Aladdin rode to the palace on a handsome horse, and the celebrations were the finest the city had ever known.

Aladdin's fame spread far and wide. It even reached the distant shores of Africa, where the evil magician had returned after failing to get the magic lamp. He believed Aladdin had died in the cave, and was wild with jealous rage when he learned that Aladdin had married the Princess. Realising that Aladdin's rise to fame must be due to the magic lamp, he decided to leave immediately for Persia and take the lamp away from Aladdin.

He arrived in the city, and set about his wicked plan.

Firstly, he bought twelve new lamps and then stood under one of the windows of Aladdin's palace to sell his wares.

"New lamps for old! New lamps for old!" he cried, hoping someone in the palace would hear him and give him the magic lamp for a new one by mistake.

Unfortunately, Aladdin had gone away for a few days, so there was every chance that the evil magician's trick would work. It did. The Princess heard him shouting outside and, not aware

"New lamps for old! New lamps for old!" shouted the magician outside the beautiful palace of Aladdin.

The slave-girl handed the lamp to the magician.

of the magic in Aladdin's old lamp, told one of her slaves to sell it.

The slave-girl called to the lamp-seller and handed him Aladdin's lamp out of the window, in exchange for a lovely shiny one.

"Well then, give me a new lamp for this old dirty one," she said laughing.

The clever magician immediately recognised the lamp and grabbed it eagerly. He quickly left the city and rubbed the lamp whereupon the Genie appeared.

"I command you, oh Genie," he snarled, "to carry Aladdin's palace and the Princess away with me to Africa."

No sooner had he told the Genie to do this, than the palace disappeared altogether.

When the Sultan discovered the loss of both his daughter and Aladdin's palace, he was so full of rage and despair that Aladdin was immediately thrown into jail. Aladdin was astonished, for he had no more idea where the palace had gone than the Sultan.

"Aladdin," ordered the Sultan, "I give you just forty days to find my poor daughter, or I shall have your head cut off!"

Aladdin left the Sultan's palace in great distress. He had no idea where to look. As he rubbed his hands in despair he touched the magic ring, and immediately the Genie appeared.

"Oh Genie, save my life and take me to my palace and beloved Princess."

The moment Aladdin spoke he was carried immediately to Africa and found himself outside the palace. Inside, one of the slaves saw him and rushed to tell the Princess. Overjoyed at seeing Aladdin again she called to him from the window, and let him in through a secret door. She told him what had happened to the lamp and how she was being kept a prisoner by the magician whom she now feared and hated.

"I have an idea," said Aladdin. "Put on your most beautiful dress and invite the magician to dinner this evening. I shall go and buy some poison."

This the Princess did, and during the meal offered the wicked magician some of her best wine, into which Aladdin had mixed some of the poisoned powder he had bought.

As the magician put down his goblet he stiffened and suddenly fell back dead in his chair. The terrible poison had done its work.

The next step was to return to Persia, but first Aladdin took the lamp from inside the magician's robe and rubbed it. Straight away the Genie appeared.

"Oh Genie," said Aladdin, "I command you to take us and our palace back to Persia."

The Genie at once obeyed, and as the sun was setting the palace whizzed through the night sky and over the roof tops until it came to rest outside the Sultan's palace.

Since the Princess had disappeared, the Sultan had been ill with grief, certain he would never see her again. Imagine his surprise when he looked out of the window, as he had done every day since she vanished, and saw the palace back again! He rushed outside and embraced them both. Such was his happiness that he ordered a great festival to celebrate their safe return.

When the Sultan died, the Princess became Queen and shared her throne with Aladdin. They were loved by everyone and reigned happily together all their lives.

The palace flew through the sky.

The Thieving Merchant

The Thieving Merchant

In the days of the great Haroun-Al-Rashid, the Caliph of Baghdad, lived an honest merchant who sold beautiful cloth to the rich people of that fabulous city. This merchant, whose name was Ali, had no wife or family and lived alone in his small house. All day he was happy selling his wares and talking to his friends in the market place. At night, however, he was disturbed by the same dream.

He saw in his dream as clearly as though the person was standing in front of him, an old man with a long white beard, dressed in cloth as beautiful as that which he sold. Each night the old man would say: "My brother, Ali, I am ashamed for you. You have not made the pilgrimage to our Holy City, Mecca, which all faithful Moslems should make."

The old man would then wag his finger at him and say:

Every night the cloth merchant saw in his dreams an old man dressed in the most beautiful cloth, and who wagged his finger at him.

The old man with a long white beard would plead with Ali to make the pilgrimage to Holy Mecca.

"I am not pleased with you and I will haunt your dreams until you make the Holy journey."

At this point, Ali would sit up, startled and wide awake, too afraid to go back to sleep again for fear that the old man would return in his dreams.

After a week of almost sleepless nights, Ali decided that he would have to make the journey to Mecca or he would never sleep again and without sleep would soon die.

This, thought Ali, is simpler said than done. What's going to happen to my business? Who's going to look after my home? These thoughts worried Ali nearly as much as the old man of his dreams. However, he knew that he must find some way to make the journey to Mecca.

After more sleepless nights Ali made up his mind to lock up his home, sell his business and take with him all his beautiful materials which he could sell on his journey. As his business was in the busiest spot in the market he had no difficulty in selling it—

Ali's friend, the merchant Hassan,
gave him the key to his storeroom.

in fact, he was paid the handsome sum of a thousand gold pieces for it.

Poor Ali, no sooner had he solved one problem than he was beset with another. What was he to do with such a large amount of money? He could not take it with him, as the road to Mecca swarmed with robbers just waiting for pilgrims like Ali. He must hide it, he thought. But where? As he walked by the potter's stall he saw a large jar. I can hide the money in this jar, he thought, so he bought the jar. The next problem was where to hide the jar. He could not hide it in his home as robbers would certainly ransack his house as soon as he left Baghdad—locked or not. No, he must find a safe place. After much thought he decided to ask his friend of many years standing and fellow merchant, Hassan, to lock the jar in his warehouse.

"My dear Hassan," said Ali, "you know that I'm making the pilgrimage to Mecca and I would be most grateful if you would let me store a jar of olives in your warehouse until I return!"

Ali trusted no one, not even his friend Hassan, so he had put his money in the jar and covered it with olives—for who would want to steal olives which were so cheap and plentiful?

"You are most welcome, my friend," replied Hassan. "I store my own olives in my warehouse. Here, take the key, open the store and place the jar anywhere you wish. When you return, you will find it just as you left it."

Ali gratefully took the key and went to the olive warehouse. There were many jars, very similar to his own, so he put his in a dark corner so that it would not be mistaken for one of Hassan's.

Now that all his affairs were settled, Ali joined a caravan and made the long pilgrimage to Mecca. There he paid homage at the famous temple of the prophet Mohammed, carrying out all the rites and ceremonies required of pilgrims. In a little while the money he had brought with him began to run out, so he rented a stall in the bazaar and displayed his fine silks and brocades.

One morning two passing merchants stopped to examine Ali's materials which, they told him, were as fine as they had ever seen. As they walked away Ali heard one merchant say to the other:

Ali joined the caravan of camels and started on the long journey to Mecca.

Ali wanted to visit all the famous Moslem temples.

"That merchant must be a fool to stay here. If he sold materials of such excellent quality in Cairo he would get ten times the price."

Being a good businessman, and because he fancied a visit to that famous capital, Ali soon packed up his stall and was on his way to Cairo. The rich Egyptians said that they had never seen such magnificent silks and paid even more than the two merchants had said. In no time Ali had sold all his stock and made a small fortune. He was in no hurry to return to Baghdad so he visited the pyramids and temples of ancient Egypt, and even went on a journey up the river Nile. As he still had a lot of money he decided to go to Damascus and then on to Jerusalem to worship at the famous Moslem temple. Even after this Ali still wanted to travel and went as far as the famous cities of India.

Seven years passed. Back in Baghdad Ali's friend, Hassan, feared that he must be dead, and had, in fact, forgotten about Ali's jar of olives.

One evening Hassan and his wife were about to have their evening meal when they discovered that they had no olives.

"Husband," said Hassan's wife, "go and get some olives from the store."

Hassan, being a dutiful husband, went to the store and was about to empty one of his own jars when he spied Ali's jar hidden away in the dark corner.

"That's Ali's jar," said Hassan aloud to himself. "He'll never be back so I might as well use his."

With this thought Hassan tipped up the jar to pour the olives into the bowl. Some mouldy olives fell out and then, to his utter amazement, out fell the thousand gold pieces. Hassan was not amazed for long. Soon greed crept into his eyes, for Hassan was well known for his miserly nature. He put the gold pieces back into the jar and again covered them with olives.

"Those olives of Ali's are rotten," he said to his wife. "If Ali doesn't return soon we shall have to throw them out."

"There's no hurry," replied his wife. "Anyway, I'm sure he will return one of these days."

All night Hassan thought about the gold pieces in Ali's jar, wondering how best he could lay his hands on them. In the morning he decided to put Ali's gold pieces in one of his own jars and hide it in his home and fill Ali's jar with fresh olives. Anyway, he felt certain that Ali would never return to Baghdad, and he would soon be able to add Ali's gold to his own hoard.

One morning several months later Hassan was walking to his shop in the market when he was very startled indeed to hear a voice shouting:

"Hassan! Hassan! It's Ali, your friend. I've returned to my beloved Baghdad."

Imagine the surprise — and dismay—on Hassan's face as Ali ran towards him.

"My dear friend, Ali, welcome home. I'm delighted to see you," said Hassan in a shaky voice. "After seven years, we all thought you would never return."

"I've been to all the great cities of the East, but there's nowhere really like one's home," mused Ali.

For some time Ali and Hassan chatted, mainly about Ali's adventures and experiences in Mecca.

When Hassan tipped up the jar a thousand gold pieces fell into his bowl.

"Well, I really should go and open up my house," said Ali, "but I'll visit your warehouse and pick up my jar of olives before I make my way home."

"I haven't the time to come with you, Ali," said Hassan. "Here is the key. You can take the jar yourself and leave the key with my wife."

Ali hurried over to the warehouse, collected his jar and returned to his old home. The first thing he did was to clean and dust, and finding himself hungry, he then prepared a meal. Feeling very contented, he brought the jar into his living room and started to scoop the olives from the top of the jar.

One scoop, two scoops, three scoops . . . ten scoops. Instantly Ali knew that something was wrong, for he had only put a few handfuls of olives

over the gold pieces. Quickly he tipped the jar upside down—but no gold pieces dropped out, only hundreds of olives. The jar contained not a single gold coin.

"Hassan has stolen my fortune," cried Ali. "And to think I always looked on him as a friend I could trust."

Grabbing the jar Ali rushed over to Hassan's house.

"Who would think my life-long friend would rob me of my money," shouted Ali at the open-mouthed—and apparently very surprised—Hassan.

"Friend, friend," retorted Hassan, "what are you accusing me of?"

"All my money was in the olive jar," cried Ali. "Now it's gone—replaced with worthless olives."

Hassan tried to look puzzled. "But you said nothing about money in the jar when you went," he protested.

"If you had need of the money, admit it," said Ali. "I will forgive you. I still have much money."

But Hassan denied that he had taken the money or had known that there was any in the jar. Instead, he said that *if* there had been money in the jar his employees must have found it and shared it between them.

Ali could see that Hassan was not going to admit taking the gold pieces.

"If you will not confess to me and return my money," said Ali, "I shall take you before the magistrate first thing tomorrow morning."

"Do as you will," replied

"Hassan! Hassan! It's Ali, your friend," cried Ali. "I've returned to my old home at last."

Ali accused his old friend, Hassan, of stealing the thousand gold pieces from his olive jar in the storeroom.

Hassan, and turned and went into his house.

Next morning Ali and Hassan appeared before the magistrate. Ali's charge that Hassan had stolen his gold pieces was read out to the magistrate.

"Have you anything to say, Hassan?" inquired the magistrate.

"Yes it is true that Ali stored his jar in my warehouse," replied Hassan. "I gave him the key to open the store and he put the jar in there himself. I didn't know where the jar was—there are so many jars in my warehouse—and I certainly didn't know there was any money hidden in it. Ali told me it contained olives and as Ali is my friend I believed what he told me."

For a few minutes the magistrate sat in silence. Then he turned to Hassan and said:

"I think you are telling the truth, Hassan. It is only right that, being a friend of Ali, you should have believed him when he told you that the jar contained olives. Case dismissed!"

Hassan rejoiced in his victory whilst Ali went home miserable and angry. But Ali was not going to let the matter drop, so the next day he went to see the wise Haroun-Al-Rashid, who promised to give the matter his fullest consideration.

That afternoon Haroun and his courtiers went for their usual walk round the streets, lanes and courts of the city. As they passed a courtyard Haroun saw a group of children heatedly talking—just like in a magistrate's court.

"What are they doing?" enquired Haroun.

"They are enacting the case of Ali and Hassan," said the Vizier. "All Baghdad is talking about it."

"Oh, are they," replied Haroun. "Let's hear what the children have to say."

"Bring me the jar of olives," said one of the boys who was sitting on a large stone. Another boy pretended to carry in the jar—in fact he held a piece of rock—whilst the boy playing the magistrate pretended to taste one of the olives.

"A lovely, fresh olive," said the boy. "However, how can this be so if Ali has been away for seven years? Any olive merchant will tell you that after three years olives go rotten and lose their flavour."

Hassan rejoiced in his victory.
Ali went home a miserable man.

Turning to the boy playing Hassan, the magistrate—really a boy of course—said:

"Hassan you have told lies. You took the money and replaced it with fresh olives. If you had used your head and used old olives you would probably never have been found out, but you were too greedy and couldn't wait to get your hands on Ali's gold."

The Caliph was delighted to discover such wisdom on a young head, and he told his Vizier to arrange for this clever boy to be at his court the very next day. Ali, Hassan, and two oil merchants were also ordered to attend Haroun's audience-hall the following morning.

When the Caliph's messenger told Ali he was to attend the audience-hall he was greatly pleased.

"Tell the Great Caliph," said the happy Ali, "that I shall be honoured to attend the audience-hall. I knew that once he heard of how unfairly I have been treated he would put matters right."

When the Caliph's messenger told Hassan to attend the audience-hall, he was not pleased, not pleased at all.

"What does the Caliph want?" said Hassan to his wife. "I've paid all my taxes."

"Perhaps he wants to buy some of your beautiful new saddles," said Hassan's wife.

"No," cried Hassan. "He would not order me to his palace just to buy saddles. It must be about Ali's gold."

"It's no use worrying until you know," said the wife. "Let's go to bed."

Poor Hassan. He did go to bed, but try as he might he didn't sleep a wink all night.

The next morning, at the appointed time, Ali and the others arrived at the Caliph's court. Haroun was already seated on his throne of office, with the boy, dressed in his best clothes, sitting on a chair beside him.

The Caliph commanded Ali and Hassan to restate their cases before the boy. This they each did, and when they had finished the boy took an olive from Ali's jar and gave it to one of the oil merchants.

"How old is this olive?" he asked the merchant.

The Great Caliph and his courtiers saw a group of children playing a game in the courtyard.

The oil merchant examined the olive carefully, smelt it and tasted it.

"It is perfectly fresh and very probably comes from this year's crop. Therefore it cannot possibly be seven years old," he said.

On hearing this, Hassan realised that all was lost. So he immediately confessed that he had stolen the gold coins and had filled the jar with fresh olives. Falling on his knees, he begged the Caliph for mercy.

"Great Caliph," Hassan cried, "have mercy on a poor merchant who let greed overcome his honesty."

"What say you Ali?" asked the Caliph.

"I do not hold any ill will against Hassan," said Ali. "All I want is the return of my thousand gold pieces. I'll then forget the incident."

"You are very generous," the Caliph said to Ali, "but we cannot overlook the crime entirely."

The Caliph then turned to his Vizier to discuss what should be done with the miserable Hassan.

Hassan realised that all was lost, and falling on his knees begged for mercy.

The Caliph orders his Vizier to give the boy a thousand pieces of gold.

Haroun was indeed merciful. Instead of having Hassan hanged, as he might well have done, he sentenced him to seven years imprisonment.

The thousand gold coins were restored to Ali, their rightful owner, and the Caliph was so pleased with the boy that he ordered the Vizier to give him a thousand pieces of gold from the Royal Treasury.

"Always take notice of what the young have to say," Haroun advised his Vizier, when it was all settled. "They are often very, very wise indeed."

The boy ran home with the bag of gold.

Ali Baba and the Forty Thieves

Ali Baba counted forty horsemen, all armed with long, sharp swords hanging from their belts. The leader shouted at the face of the rock: "Open Sesame!"

Long ago in Persia, there lived two brothers—Cassim and Ali Baba. Their father had recently died, and not being a rich man, had left only a small inheritance to be divided equally between them. For a while they each lived quite humbly, but before very long a great change came in both their lives.

Cassim, who was the elder, married a woman who owned a great deal of property in the district, and whose father was very well-off. Thanks to his wife, Cassim became one of the richest merchants in the city. Ali Baba, on the other hand, married a woman who was just as poor as himself. They had to live in a tiny, bare house and eat the plainest food. Ali Baba earned what he could as a wood-cutter. Every day he went to the nearby forest to chop wood, and in the evening he would carry it into the city on the backs of his three asses and sell it in the market-place.

One summer day in the forest, Ali Baba, who had chopped as much wood as his asses could carry, leant back against the trunk of a tree in order to rest for a few moments and gather strength for the journey back to the city. Suddenly he noticed a cloud of dust on the horizon, and soon

he found that the cloud was getting nearer and that he could hear the faint beat of horses' hooves. Gradually the shapes of many men on horses became clear through the dust, and Ali Baba could see that they were riding straight towards him.

Now Ali Baba was a cautious man, and although that part of the country was not supposed to be dangerous he suspected that these horsemen might be a band of thieves. Frightened by what they might do to him, and forgetting his poor asses, he looked around desperately for somewhere to hide. A tall tree grew nearby at the foot of a steep rock, so he hurriedly climbed up into its thick, leafy branches. Here he could watch everything below, without anyone seeing him. The riders were now almost upon him, and he could see their savage, bearded faces as they spurred on their horses. Then he remembered his asses! "I only hope they have strayed away and the robbers don't see them," he thought.

The horsemen galloped up and stopped right underneath Ali Baba's tree. He counted forty of them in all. They were fierce-looking and well armed. Long, sharp swords hung from their belts, and Ali Baba was now certain they were a band of dangerous robbers. Keeping perfectly still and quiet, he watched each rider dismount and take the bridle off his horse. The animal was then given a bag of barley to eat and tethered to a nearby bush. The robbers unloaded their saddle-bags and hurriedly carried them to the foot of the rock. The bags appeared to be so heavy that Ali Baba was convinced they were full of some heavy metal—gold, perhaps, or silver. At that moment, a tall, bearded man, dressed in a red cloak, came forward towards the rock beside the very tree in which Ali Baba was hiding. From his dress and his grim looks Ali Baba decided that this man must be the leader of the band. The robber chief brushed his way through the bushes and shrubs to the face of the rock and suddenly cried out, in a loud voice: "Open, Sesame!"

No sooner had he said this than a great stone door swung open in the rock face revealing the entrance to a vast cave. The band quickly entered and the door closed silently after them.

Now Ali Baba was only an ordinary woodcutter. He had heard plenty about robbers before, but as for magic doorways in rocks—he had never believed in such things. So naturally he was very, very surprised by what he had seen, and frightened too. "Good Heavens," he said to himself, "if their chief can open doors with magic commands, what would he do to me if he caught me prying into his secrets? I don't suppose he would hesitate to kill me on the spot so that no one else

The robbers carried bags of gold and caskets of jewels into the cave.

should find out about his cave."

Ali Baba wondered if he should climb down from the tree while the robbers were inside the rock and run home as fast as his feet would carry him. But he decided that this would be unwise, for the robbers might come out of the cave at any moment. In fact, the robbers stayed in the cave for a long time, so poor Ali Baba was forced to sit in his tree and wait patiently for them to reappear. All the while, he kept his eyes glued on the cave entrance, waiting for something to happen.

Ali Baba kept perfectly still and quiet and watched the robbers go into the cave.

At last the great door of the cave opened and the forty thieves came out, with their leader in front. When he had made sure the cave was empty, Ali Baba heard him say:

"Shut, Sesame!" Sure enough the door closed at once.

Each man then went to his horse, put on its bridle and fastened on the saddle-bags. When their leader saw that they were all ready to depart, he rode to the front and all the band galloped off along the same road by which they had arrived.

Ali Baba watched them ride into the distance until they were completely out of sight. He didn't move for a long while after the clouds of dust had settled and the hoof beats could no longer be heard, in case they had forgotten something and decided to come back. But at last he climbed down from the tree and stretched his aching legs. He could still hardly believe what had happened and, had it not been for the pain in his legs, he might have thought he had been dreaming.

As a small boy, Ali Baba had always been rather curious about things, and now he was very curious about the cave. "I wonder if it would open for me?" he asked himself. "And I wonder what I would find if I went inside, too?" He was still rather frightened that the robbers might return, but the fascination of the cave was too great for him. So he walked quickly over to the rock and looked for the door, but there were no cracks to be seen. Fortunately he remembered the magic words the robber chief had used, and he decided to try them out for himself.

"Open, Sesame!" he cried, in a loud voice. Immediately, the door swung open for him. Ali Baba stood open-mouthed with amazement. What a secret he had discovered! No one would ever believe this had happened to him. Still trembling with excitement, he decided to enter the cave and explore it.

Ali Baba peeped inside. He had expected the cave to be dark and gloomy and was amazed to find a large, well-lit chamber hewn out of the rock. It was too high for him to touch the roof with his hand. The light entered through a hole in the roof and the dazzling sight which it revealed left Ali Baba breathless with wonder. Before him was more treasure than he thought could exist in the whole world. It was like some vast royal treasure chamber. Stacked before him were bales of expensive coloured silks and brocades, and gold and silver coins, some piled high in gleaming heaps and the rest filling hundreds of leather sacks on the cave floor. There were diamond necklaces, strings of pearls, basins full of emeralds and rubies, solid gold vases and goblets and priceless carpets. The treasure filled the whole cave, from wall to wall and from ceiling to floor. Even forty thieves could not have gathered all this. It must have been a robbers' treasure chest for centuries.

Ali Baba now walked right inside the cavern and, as soon as he had passed through the entrance, the door slammed shut behind him. As he had remembered the two magic words which would make it open again, he was not at all afraid.

Ali Baba decided that he would take as much of the treasure as he could manage to carry on the backs of his three asses. He would have to leave

Ali Baba was dazzled by all the treasures. Never had he seen so much gold and silver. Also there were jewels and bales of coloured silks and brocades.

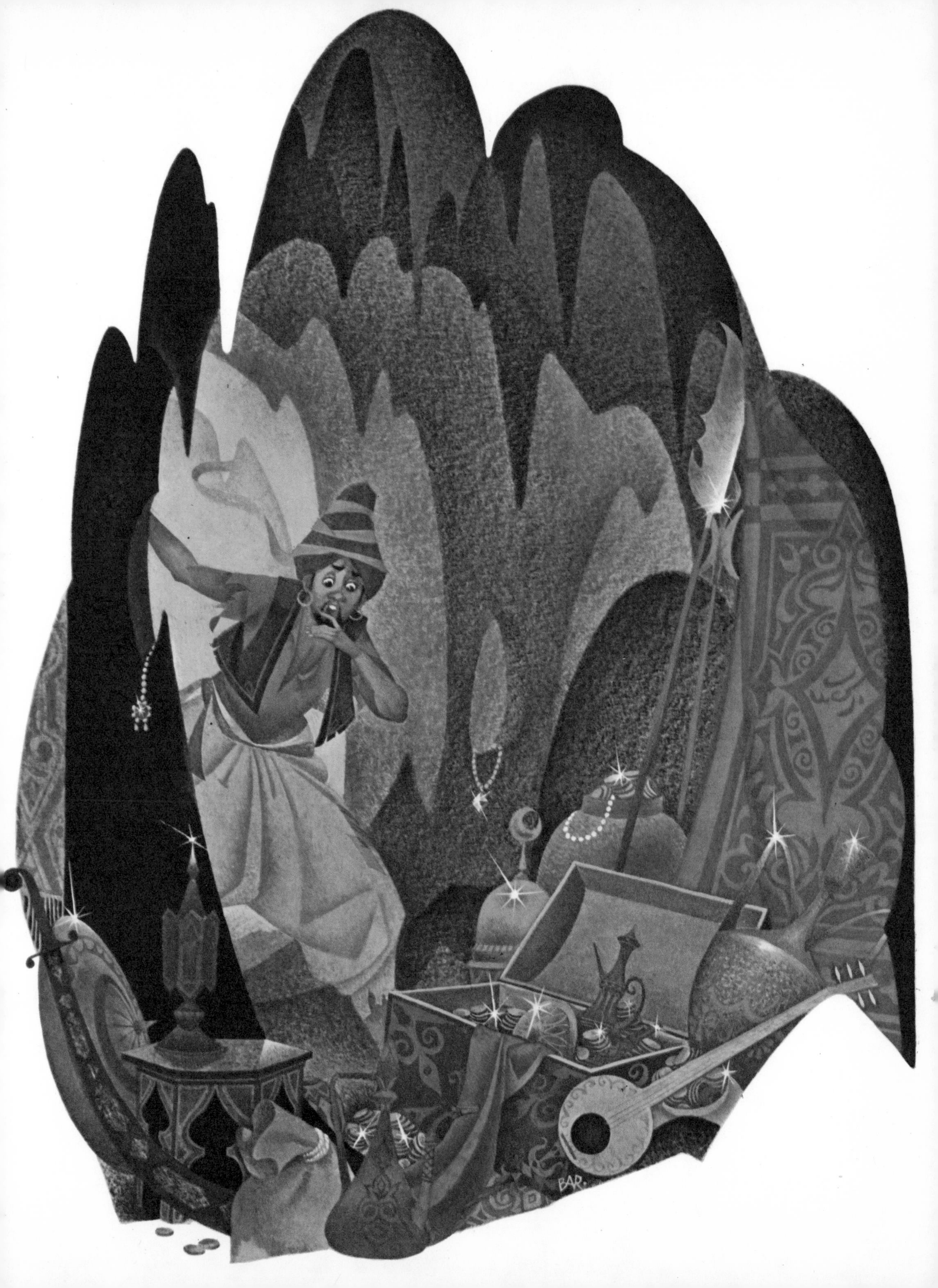
BAR

plenty behind in the cavern, but he could take enough to make his family very rich—far richer than his brother Cassim. They would be able to buy a new house in a better part of the city and all have fine new clothes and plenty of food. Ali Baba looked around carefully to see what would be the best treasures to take. The silver plates and cutlery would be too heavy and bulky, and Ali Baba—who knew nothing about jewels—wasn't sure which precious stones would be the most valuable. So he decided to collect as many gold coins as he could and transport them in their leather sacks on the backs of his asses.

Soon Ali Baba had collected as much as he thought his asses could carry and, after commanding the door of the cave to open, he went in search of the beasts. He brought them round to the cave door and loaded them high with the heavy sacks of gold. So that no one would see the sacks, Ali Baba carefully covered them with the twigs and wood he had chopped earlier in the day. He then went up to the cave door and cried: "Shut, Sesame!" The door silently closed and Ali Baba set off as fast as he could.

Ali Baba loaded his asses with sacks of gold coins and covered them with wood so that they would not be seen on his way home.

Ali Baba was a silent man on his journey back to his home. What, he thought, would his wife say to such wealth, and, more, what would his brother Cassim say—and his greedy wife? Ali Baba also thought of his friends, and if his new found wealth would make them so envy him that he would lose their friendship. Poor Ali Baba, although he now had found great wealth he was still worried.

Ali Baba could not believe his eyes.

With his newfound wealth Ali Baba would be able to buy a magnificent new house for his poor family.

Ali Baba went to Cassim's house
and begged his wife to lend him a weighing pan.

When he reached home he quickly unloaded the bulging sacks of gold and carried them into his house. His wife was waiting for him and couldn't understand what was going on. She tried to pick up one of the sacks, but it was too heavy for her. Then, when she looked inside and saw the gold coins, she became frightened.

"Oh! Ali Baba," she said, in tears, "surely you haven't turned into a thief?"

"Now, now, don't be upset," her husband replied comfortingly. "You will know the truth in a minute and learn of our good fortune."

As he emptied the contents of the sacks onto the floor, Ali Baba told his wife exactly what had happened to him in the forest, and made her promise to tell no-one.

"Otherwise," he said, "we shall have Cassim going out to the cave, and the robbers would be sure to catch him. Now we must hide this treasure before anyone sees it. You count the money while I go to borrow a weighing pan from my brother Cassim. I'm dying to know how much gold is there! Remember, not a word to anyone."

Ali Baba set off for his brother's house, which was not far away. Cassim was out, so Ali Baba begged Cassim's wife to lend him a weighing pan.

"Certainly. Wait just a minute while I go and find it," she said.

Unfortunately, Cassim's wife was suspicious. She wondered what it was that Ali Baba wanted to weigh; for she knew he was a woodcutter, and you don't weigh wood in a weighing pan. So she stuck some glue to the bottom of the pan before she gave it to him.

When Ali Baba weighed the gold he was astonished to find how heavy and valuable it was, and he returned the pan to his sister-in-law in a hurry without examining it. Cassim's wife thanked Ali in a very friendly way, but as soon as she had shut the door she hastily examined the pan and found a gold coin stuck inside it.

Cassim's wife was a jealous person, always wanting to be richer than everyone else. The thought that her poor brother-in-law now had so much gold that he found it simpler to weigh it than to count it made her very angry. When her husband returned home she turned on him in a furious temper.

"What is it?" asked the startled Cassim.

"You fool, Cassim," she cried, "you think you are rich, but Ali Baba has deceived you! He pretends to be poor, but he is far

Cassim, Ali Baba's brother, demanded to know how much gold his brother had and that he should share it.

richer than you, for instead of counting his money as you do, he has so much that he has to weigh it." Then she told him about the pan and the gold coin.

Cassim became furious. He rushed over to his brother's house and burst in on him, waving the pan.

"So, Ali Baba," shouted Cassim nastily, "you are very secretive about your affairs. While we all think you are poor, you actually have so much money that you have to weigh it."

"What do you mean?" asked Ali Baba.

"You know very well," cried Cassim, holding up the pan containing the piece of gold. "How many more of these do you have?"

Realising that his secret had been discovered, Ali Baba knew that it was useless to try to conceal the truth any longer. So he told Cassim everything about the robbers' cave and how he had found the treasure. He even offered to share the treasure with his brother if he promised to tell no one.

"And so you should share it," snapped Cassim, ungratefully. "If you don't tell me immediately where the cave is and how to open it, I shall go out at once and tell everyone your secret."

So Ali Baba gave away even these last two secrets. The next morning, the greedy Cassim set off for the cave with ten mules, intending to take all the treasure for himself. When he found the right spot, he jumped down from his horse and ran to the rock.

"Open, Sesame!" he shouted. The door of the cave opened just as Ali Baba had said it would, and closed behind him after he entered.

When Cassim first saw all the treasure gleaming in front of him, he could hardly believe his eyes, but he soon began to drag sack after sack to the cave entrance, chuckling to himself with greedy delight. Now he was ready to open the door.

"Open Barley!" he shouted. Nothing happened! He had completely forgotten the magic words. Panic stricken, he threw himself to the floor. His selfish greed had made him a prisoner in the cave.

Later that afternoon the thieves returned and saw the mules outside the cave. They were on their guard at once and, drawing their swords and daggers, rushed into the cave and found the frightened Cassim. He tried to escape, but there was no way out. The thieves grabbed him and put him to death on the spot.

The thieves could not understand, however, how Cassim had got into the cave. The hole in the roof was too high and too narrow for such a fat man to squeeze through, and it did not seem possible that he could have discovered the magic words. To frighten off any further intruders, they cut poor Cassim's body into quarters and placed it inside the entrance. Then, mounting their horses, they rode off in search of further plunder.

Meanwhile, Cassim's wife, worried because her husband had not

The thieves rushed into the cave and found the frightened Cassim. He tried to escape but there was no way out. Cassim was executed on the spot.

Cassim's wife broke down and cried when she was told of her husband's death.

returned, went to Ali Baba in great distress to ask for his help.

"Your brother Cassim has not returned. He went off to the cave this morning. Something must have happened to him!"

Ali Baba said Cassim would surely return before it was dark. But sunset came, and Cassim still had not returned. Ali Baba now began to worry too, and agreed to set off first thing in the morning to find his brother.

As Ali Baba approached the rock door, he was horrified to see bloodstains. Trembling with fear, he opened the cave and saw what had become of poor Cassim's body. Ali Baba was very shocked. He lifted his brother's body onto his ass and covered it with sacks and wood. Then he commanded the cave door to close and set off for home quickly, afraid that the thieves might return and do the same to him.

When Ali Baba broke the news to Cassim's wife she broke down and cried, and it was a long while before he could get her to listen to him.

"I know what a great shock this is," said Ali Baba, consolingly, "but it is important that everyone should think that Cassim died naturally or they will discover our secret. I have a plan, but to carry it out I need the help of your slave Morgiana."

Morgiana led the blindfolded cobbler to the house of the now-dead Cassim.

The next day, Morgiana was sent to speak to the local cobbler, Mustapha.

"Look, Mustapha," she said, "here is some money. In return, bring your needles and cotton and come with me. I must first bandage your eyes, for you must not know where we are going. Tell no one, and you have no need to be afraid."

Only when the pair reached Cassim's house were Mustapha's eyes uncovered.

"If you sew these four quarters together," said Morgiana, pointing to Cassim's body, "and keep it a secret, you can have another piece of gold."

Mustapha did as he was told, and was very handsomely rewarded. Afterwards he was led back to his workshop with his eyes bandaged as before. Once Cassim had been properly buried, no one suspected how he had really met his death.

Meanwhile, the forty thieves had discovered to their horror the disappearance of Cassim's body, and of part of their treasure.

"Someone else knows about the cave," said their leader at last. "Obviously the rascal we caught was not the only one who knew. To protect our secret we must find the other rogue at once and kill him."

All the thieves were in agreement, of course.

"First, one of you who is brave and clever must go to the city disguised as a traveller to find out whether people are talking about the horrible way the rascal we caught died. He must discover who the man was and where he lived. Should the one who is chosen fail, let him be put to death!"

The thieves were so greedy for revenge that all thirty-nine offered to go. But at last one was singled out and he set off very early for the city. He found only one shop open—Mustapha the cobbler's shop.

"Goodness!" he said to Mustapha, "how do you manage to sew so neatly when your eyes are so old?"

"I may be old," replied Mustapha, "but my eyes are excellent. A few hours ago I even stitched up a dead body so you would never have known the poor wretch didn't die in one piece."

"Show me where you did such wonderful sewing," said the

One of the thieves visited the shop of the cobbler, Mustapha, to find out where Cassim had lived.

robber, chuckling with delight at his luck, and he offered the cobbler a large bag of gold.

"Well," said Mustapha, "I can only guess the direction as I had my eyes bandaged while I was led there."

Nevertheless, he managed to guide the robber through the streets, guessing the way Morgiana had led him, and eventually he stopped right in front of Cassim's house, which Ali Baba now lived in.

"I am sure I went no further than this," said Mustapha.

While Mustapha was looking the other way, the robber quickly marked a white cross on the door so that he would recognise it again when he came back with his leader. He thanked the cobbler for his information, gave him two more pieces of gold, leapt on to his horse, and galloped off towards the forest. How pleased his leader would be, he thought.

Just after Mustapha and the robber had left the street, Morgiana had to go out to buy some fruit. On her return, she noticed

The robber marked a white cross on the door of Cassim's house to make sure of it when he returned.

The leader of the robbers danced with anger when he realised he had been fooled.

the white cross on the door.

"What does this mean?" she asked herself. "Is someone playing a practical joke on my master? I know how to confuse them if they are!"

She fetched a piece of white chalk and marked a cross on all the other doors in the street so that they looked exactly the same. Then she went inside to prepare a meal, and told no one what she had done.

The robber, meanwhile, had reached the forest and rejoined his friends. He told them of the success of his journey and they clapped and cheered with delight. The next step, they decided, was for the leader and he to return to the city and find out more about the house. As soon as the decision had been taken, they both left for the city and the spy led his leader to the street where he had marked the door with chalk. Imagine his astonishment when he saw a whole row of doors, each marked with a white cross.

"I must be dreaming," he stammered in dismay. "I only marked one door, and now I cannot tell which one it was."

The robbers' leader was merciless when one of his men failed him. He made the robber gallop back to the camp, and told the others what had happened. They had no hesitation in deciding what to do. They cut his head off before he could even protest.

Another robber was appointed in his place to discover who knew their secret, but he too lost his head in the end. For Morgiana's sharp eyes spotted the door he had marked in red, so that when the leader arrived, there was a whole row of doors with red crosses on them.

Now there were only thirty-eight robbers left. Their leader decided that he could not afford to lose any more men, so he jumped onto his horse

Morgiana marked a cross on other doors in the street so that they looked exactly the same.

and went off to investigate for himself. With Mustapha's help he found the right door, but instead of marking it with chalk, he memorised it in every detail until he was sure he could recognise it another time. Then he went back to the forest, summoned his band, and told them of his plan.

They were to steal some asses and carts, and thirty-eight large jars for carrying oil. One jar was to be full of oil, the others empty, and all the jars were to be loaded onto the carts. Each man, except the leader, was to collect his weapons and hide himself inside a jar. The leader would close each jar so that it appeared to be full of oil, leaving a small gap to allow the man inside to breathe. Finally, to make it look as though all the jars were full of oil, he would rub the outsides with a little oil. The leader would disguise himself in the clothes of an oil merchant, and lead the carts and the mules into the city.

Everything went according to plan. The robbers arrived in the city and their leader went to knock at the door of Ali Baba's house and ask for shelter for himself and his mules. As Ali Baba was sitting on his doorstep

The leader of the robbers knocked at Ali Baba's door and asked for shelter for himself and his mules.

enjoying the cool evening air after supper, the robber stopped and spoke to him.

"Good sir," he said, "I have brought my jars of oil a long way to sell in the market tomorrow, and it is so late that I cannot find a place to stay. May I spend the night in your house?"

Although Ali Baba had seen the leader of the robbers at the cave, and had even heard him shout "Open, Sesame!", he failed to recognise him now, for he was so well disguised.

"You are most welcome, Sir," said Ali Baba kindly, and he invited the robber chief inside.

The mules and carts were taken round to the courtyard at the back of the house. The carts were unloaded and the mules were fed. Morgiana was asked to prepare some food for their guest and to make him up for the night. When he had eaten, Ali Baba showed his guest to his room and wished him goodnight.

While Ali Baba returned to his hearth, the robber chief slipped out into

In each jar was an armed robber waiting to kill Ali Baba.

the dark courtyard to tell his men what they had to do. Going to each jar in turn, he whispered inside:

"When I throw some stones from the window of my room, jump out of the jar with your knife at the ready. I shall be waiting to give you your orders."

Morgiana was making a pot of soup in the kitchen for the next day when the oil lamp began to go out. There was no oil in the house, but she knew there was plenty of oil in the merchant's jars which he had left in the courtyard, and she went out to fill the lamp. As she drew near the first jar, she was astonished to hear a voice from inside it say:

"Is it time to come out yet?"

Now Morgiana was very clever. Understanding that there were men inside the jars instead of oil, she realised at once that her master was in great danger. So she thought quickly, and then answered in a whisper:

"Not yet, but soon."

She went to each jar and found that there was only one jar of oil and thirty-seven men! How should she deal with these villains? She heated the oil from the jar on the kitchen fire, and then poured enough of the boiling liquid into each jar to stifle and kill the man inside. When this was done she returned to the kitchen and waited to see what would happen next.

It wasn't long before the leader of the robbers awoke. He got up, opened the window and looked out. All was dark and quiet. He gave the signal as arranged, and listened. Nothing moved at all! He dropped stones onto the jars a second and a third time, but still none of the robbers appeared. Filled with suspicion, he crept from his room down into the courtyard.

Morgiana heated the jar of oil on the kitchen fire and poured the boiling liquid into each jar.

The leader of the robbers rushed from jar to jar, only to discover that every one of his robber band was dead. There was nothing for him to do but make fast his escape.

As he approached the first jar, he noticed a strong smell of hot oil. Now he feared the worst. He rushed desperately from jar to jar, only to discover that every one of his faithful band was dead. Though filled with hatred and fury, he knew he had been outwitted this time. There was nothing he could do but escape as fast as he could, and then make a new plan to revenge himself on Ali Baba.

When Morgiana saw the robber creep stealthily out through the back gate, she imagined that he was so frightened that he had decided to escape while he could. Naturally, she felt very pleased with herself, for she thought she had seen the last of the robbers; so she locked the doors and went to bed.

Next morning, when Ali Baba came down to breakfast, Morgiana led him to one of the oil jars in the courtyard and asked him to look inside.

"Morgiana!" he gasped, "there is a dead man in here. What is the meaning of this?"

Morgiana explained what had happened: how Ali Baba had been in great danger, and how she had killed the robbers.

"Oh! Morgiana," cried Ali Baba, with tears in his eyes, "you have saved my life. You shall cease to be a slave at once, and shall live in my house in freedom. Come! Let us bury these bodies quickly in the garden and hide the oil jars and weapons. I shall sell the mules and carts tomorrow to avoid suspicion."

Unfortunately, Ali Baba did not realise that he was still in grave danger.

The leader of the thieves returned to the forest mad with rage at the failure of his plan. He believed that the clever Ali Baba was responsible for the deaths of all his men, and was more determined than ever to kill him. He decided to act quickly. Next day, he set out for the city again, taking with him much fine linen and expensive materials, and he set himself up as a rich merchant in a new shop. Just by chance, his shop happened to be opposite the one where Ali Baba's son David worked. The robber pretended that his name was Houssain, and started to make friends with the neighbours.

One day, Ali Baba's son went to Houssain's shop to buy some silk, and the two of them gradually became friendly. As they got to know each other better, David happened to mention that his father was named Ali Baba. The evil robber saw that a lucky chance had brought him the opportunity he had been waiting for to get rid of Ali Baba once and for all. So, almost every day, he made an effort to see David, gave him gifts, and soon began inviting him to his home

Ali Baba's son, David, went to Houssain's shop to buy some silk and mentioned that his father was Ali Baba.

to dine. He was so clever in the way he did this, and his friendship appeared so genuine, that David never once suspected his wicked intentions.

As David was polite and kind-hearted like his father, he felt he had to return Houssain's hospitality. He had very little money of his own and asked his father what he should do.

"Well, David," said his father, "tomorrow is Friday, and the merchants' shops will be closed all day. I have heard so much about your friend Houssain that I should very much like to meet him. Why don't you invite him here for dinner, tomorrow evening at seven?"

The next day the robber found himself invited to dine in the house of the man he planned to kill. What a piece of luck! But the crafty Houssain knew how clever Ali Baba was, and was rather afraid of his dinner, in case his host tried to poison him. He told David that he would be very pleased to come, but not to dine, because his food had to be specially cooked without salt.

"If this is his only reason," said Ali Baba to David, "I insist that he still dine with us, and I promise you that all the food he eats will be cooked without salt. I will see to it myself."

The robber was unable to refuse the invitation to dinner. Ali Baba told Morgiana not to put any salt in the meat she was going to serve for supper, or in

Morgiana danced more gracefully than she had ever done, and gradually drew out the two daggers.

As a reward for her services, Ali Baba allowed Morgiana and his son to marry.

any of the other dishes. She could not help being surprised at Ali Baba's request.

"Who is this strange man who eats meat without salt?" she asked.

"He is a good, honest man, and a friend of David," replied Ali Baba.

When Morgiana carried in the food she immediately recognised Houssain as the leader of the robbers, and noticed that he had a dagger partly concealed under his robe. Obviously Ali Baba was in great danger! What could she do?

At that same moment, the robber was making his final plans.

"If I can get them both drunk," he thought cunningly, "David will not be able to stop me when I plunge the dagger into his father's heart. Then I shall escape through the garden while the serving-girl is in the kitchen."

"Friend of my son," said Ali Baba, "I trust the food was to your liking?"

"Ali Baba, father of my friend David," replied Houssain, "everything was excellent. My own cook could not have done better."

"Is there anything else you would care for?" asked Ali Baba, always a considerate host.

"No, good friend," answered Houssain, whose thoughts were concentrated on the death of his 'good friend.' "

"If you wish," continued Ali Baba, "I will ask the musicians to play so that you may relax."

"An excellent idea," said Houssain. "Perhaps you have some servants who can dance for us?"

Houssain's idea was to kill Ali Baba whilst everyone was watching the dancing.

Morgiana acted quickly. Instead of remaining in the kitchen, she dressed herself as a dancing girl, and concealed two small daggers in her sash. She entered the room where Ali Baba and Houssain were dining and begged Ali Baba to allow her to dance for his guest.

"What an excellent idea, Morgiana," laughed Ali Baba. "You shall see what a wonderful dancer she is, Houssain."

So Morgiana began to dance more gracefully than she had ever danced before, and, as if it were part of her dance, she gradually drew out the two daggers and waved them in the air. At the same time she watched Houssain, and noticed that he had moved his hand to his own dagger. Quickly, she twirled towards him, and then plunged one of her daggers into his heart.

Ali Baba started back with horror as his guest fell dead to the floor.

"Morgiana!" he cried, wringing his hands. "What have you done? Houssain was our guest. I shall be ruined."

"What I have done was for your own safety," she replied, and, pointing to the dagger in the robber's robe, explained who Houssain really was.

"Once again, Morgiana," said the grateful Ali Baba, "I owe you my life. To show you how thankful I am, you shall become my son David's wife."

A few days later, David and Morgiana were happily married. Ali Baba, too, lived happily and peacefully for the rest of his life. He gave much of his riches to the poor, and the whole city loved and honoured him dearly.

The
Voyages
of
Sindbad

BAR.

Hindbad, the poor porter, sat down to rest in the shade of a tree and mopped his brow.

Once upon a time in the city of Baghdad, there lived a very poor porter named Hindbad. One hot summer day he was carrying a heavy load through the city and, wearied by the intense heat, he sat down to rest in the shade of a tree. As he was mopping his forehead, he noticed a beautiful white house in front of him. From the windows came the sound of music and the smell of delicious food. Curious to know who the rich owner was, he went to ask one of the servants.

'What!' replied the servant, 'do you not know that Sindbad the Sailor lives here!'

Knowing how wealthy Sindbad was, Hindbad exclaimed bitterly: 'Oh Allah, look at the difference between Sindbad and myself. I have hardly enough money to buy bread each day, but he is so rich that he can have everything he wants. Why is he so lucky? Do I deserve to be so poor?'

Just then the servant invited Hindbad inside to meet his master. Surprised, but afraid that Sindbad might have heard his complaining, he entered. He was led into a large, richly decorated room and, trembling with fright, was introduced to his host. Sindbad was old and sat on a throne of cushions in front of a group of guests.

'Come, I am happy to see you,' said Sindbad. 'I could not help hearing what you said outside. If you think I won my riches easily, you are mistaken. I had to endure great suffering on seven terrible voyages across the seas. Listen and I shall now tell you of the dangers I had to face!'

'As a young man, I thought only of pleasure and I wasted the fortune my father had left me. Realising how foolish I had been, I decided to use the rest of this money to become a trader and roam the seas. I soon set sail for the East Indies with some merchants.

'One day when the sea was very calm, we saw a small island in the distance and thought this was an excellent spot to stop. The captain gave us permission to go ashore, and ordered the sails to be lowered. Whilst we were enjoying ourselves eating and relaxing after our long journey, however, the island suddenly moved and began to shake! The island was

Trembling with fright, Hindbad sat in the magnificent room.

Sindbad set sail for the East Indies with some merchants.

no island at all, but the back of a gigantic whale! Some of us jumped into the sea in a panic, others drowned. I was still on top of the whale when it dived below the surface. Terrified, I only had time to grab a piece of floating wood which we had brought with us to make a fire, when the huge whale suddenly disappeared down into the depths of the ocean.

'Our captain was anxious to escape and sailed away without me. I clung to the piece of wood all that day and night, and grew very weak. The next morning, I found myself on dry land, and realised that I was on an island and out of danger!

'I washed in a fresh stream and decided to explore the island. I came to a beautiful plain where some very fine horses were grazing. Whilst I was admiring them a man came up to me and asked me who I was. He took me to a cave full of other people, who were all astonished to see me and hear of my adventure.

'I was given food, and I asked these people who they were. I learned that they were grooms to the king of the island and they brought the horses I had seen to graze on the island only one day in each year. So, if I had arrived a day later, I would not have met them and would certainly have died.

The island was no island at all, but the back of a whale which had come to the surface.

'The following day they returned to their capital to take the horses to their king, and I went along with them. When I met their king he took pity on me, and ordered that I be given everything I needed. I was supplied with new clothes and money to set me on my way.

'At the quay I noticed a ship's crew unloading some valuable packages, and recognised this cargo as my own! I rushed up to the captain who was astonished to see me alive, for this was the man who had sailed off and left me to die. Soon, with my valuable cargo, we set sail for home.

'Although I made up my mind to spend the rest of my days in Baghdad, it was not long before my desire to travel and see foreign lands made me leave on a second voyage, roaming the seas as a trader once more.

'One day we landed on a strange island where there were only fruit trees growing. We could find no trace of houses or human beings. Whilst my companions went to gather fruit I fell asleep by a stream. I cannot say how long I was asleep but when I awoke all my friends had gone! Alarmed at this I ran to look for them and saw our ship sailing away on the horizon.

'I decided to look for food and shelter, and climbed to the top of a high tree to study the land around me. Gazing out, I noticed a curious large white object in the distance. On going to examine it, I found a white ball

Sindbad grabbed a piece of wood.

The king of the island took pity on poor Sindbad and gave him new clothes and money.

of enormous size. Suddenly the sky grew very dark, which surprised me, and then I saw the reason why. A gigantic bird was flying towards me, and the white object was its egg!

'When I saw the huge brown bird in the sky I was so frightened that I ran to hide near the egg. As the roc landed beside me, one of its huge claws was very near to where I stood. It was as large as a tree trunk. With the red linen of my turban I fastened myself securely to its claw, hoping that when the bird flew away it would carry me from that

Sindbad climbed a tree and found a white object of enormous size. It was the egg of the giant bird.

deserted island.

'My plan worked, for when the roc flew off it carried me so high that I grew dizzy and could no longer see the earth below. It flew at this height for some time, then dived so suddenly that I almost fainted with shock. When it eventually landed I quickly untied the knot which bound me to its foot and hid behind a rock. I was grateful that the bird had not seen or felt me on its claw for it would certainly have gobbled me up! Then it seized a huge snake in its beak and flew away.

'The roc had left me in a deep valley surrounded by mountains which were so steep and high that it was impossible for me to climb up them. I noticed that the rocks were strewn with astonishingly large diamonds which made me excited. But soon my joy turned into fear and horror, for in the distance I saw a mass of enormous snakes. During the day they hid in the caves from their enemy, the roc, and only came out at night. Cold and sad, I hid from them in the caves at night. At sunrise the snakes crawled back

Sindbad filled a bag with the largest diamonds he could find and tied himself to the giant bird with his turban.

to their caves and, trembling, I left mine. I was so frightened that I had no wish to possess the diamonds lying around me.

'One afternoon I fell asleep, but was quickly woken by the noise of something falling. It was a large piece of meat! I realised that this was the famous Valley of Diamonds, and that the stories of how merchants gathered the stones were really true. They threw down large lumps of meat which stuck to some of the diamonds. When the eagles seized these pieces of meat, they carried them up to their young and then the merchants drove the birds from their nests to collect the precious gems. This gave me an idea. Filling my bag with the largest diamonds I could find, I tied myself to a large piece of meat with my turban and lay quite still. Soon I was seized by an eagle and carried up to its nest. There, the merchants rescued me and I told them my incredible story. They helped me return to Baghdad with my diamond fortune.

'I stayed in Baghdad for some time but soon grew weary of doing nothing, and forgetting the dangers of my previous journeys, I left on my third voyage.

'One day, our ship was driven off course by a violent storm which carried us towards an island where we dropped anchor. Our captain warned us that this island was inhabited by a savage race of dwarfs. Suddenly we saw them storming the ship—red-haired monkey-like creatures about two feet high!

'We were terrified and helpless and our ship was dragged ashore. We were forced to jump onto the land and marched to a beautiful palace. When the gates of the courtyard were opened we were horrified to see piles of human bones. Suddenly, a huge fat black giant appeared as tall and as strong as a tree. His front teeth were long and yellow and very sharp, and his mouth was enormous. His ears reached down to his shoulders!

'At the sight of this terrifying giant, we almost fainted with fright. He seized us all in turn to examine us, and then prodded us all over to see who would make a tasty meal. Suddenly he grabbed our poor captain, who was the fattest, and ate him for supper! Then he went off to bed where he slept until morning.

'All means of escaping seemed impossible. The next evening the wicked giant ate another of us. We were all in despair and then I thought of a plan.

'There was some drift wood on the beach which I suggested we use to build rafts. Everyone thought this an excellent idea and we rushed to the shore the next morning. When the rafts were finished we hid them behind rocks.

'In order to deal with the giant,

Sindbad's joy turned to fear and horror, for he saw a mass of serpents.

we had, unfortunately to wait until he had eaten yet another of us before we could do anything. We made sure he was fast asleep and waited until he was snoring loudly and then crept one by one down to the beach as silently as we could. We had to wait until dawn before setting sail, three men on each raft.

'Just after we had put to sea, we saw to our horror that the giant was running towards the shore! We rowed away as furiously as possible, but he picked up huge boulders and hurled them at us. He sank every raft except the one we were on, and we were the only survivors.

'Thankful for our escape, we rowed with all our strength and were soon far out on the open sea. We then had the good fortune to be washed up on an island which we found rich in fresh fruit and water.

Suddenly the ship was stormed by savage red-haired monkey-like creatures about two feet high.

The giant seized all the crew in turn to see if they would make a meal.

'That night we slept on the shore but were awakened by the hissing of a gigantic serpent. It was already gobbling up one of my companions, so we both ran to climb the highest tree we could find. But the serpent was so long that it rose up and ate my other companion and then crawled away. I wondered why it had not eaten me!

'Unable to believe that I was still alive, I rushed to the cliffs next morning and sat on the highest rock. There the snake could not reach me, although it tried to eat me many times. Suddenly I spotted a ship and cried out, waving my turban in the air. Luckily the captain saw me and sent a boat to take me off the island. This was the captain who had left me asleep on my second voyage. He returned my precious cargo from that trip to me,

and together we returned to the port of Basra and then onto Baghdad.

'Yet again I tired of a life of luxury, and left on my fourth voyage. Everything went well until a storm wrecked our ship and most of the crew and cargo were lost. Some of us managed to grab pieces of wood and were washed up onto an island. Within minutes savage natives had captured us. They offered us food to eat, but I was suspicious of this sudden kindness and refused, although my companions ate greedily. I was right, for soon the food made them drowsy, and when we were given bowls of rice I realised that these people were cannibals and intended to eat us when they had fattened us up!

The giant picked up a huge boulder and flung it down on the raft.

'Meanwhile, I was allowed to go where I pleased in the village and one day I escaped. I lived on coconuts and any fruit I could find, until one day I saw some people on the shore. When I spoke to them I found they were from another island, to which they kindly took me.

'There, they led me to their king, who was amazed at my adventure. We soon became good friends. I noticed, however, that no one on the island rode with a saddle, bridle or stirrups. When I asked his majesty why not, he had never heard of such things! So I made him a leather saddle which I embroidered with gold, and some stirrups and bridles. I showed him how to use them and gave him them as a present. He

The huge serpent was so long that it rose up and ate Sindbad's companion.

was so delighted that in return he gave me a rich beautiful lady for my wife.

'One day the wife of one of my friends suddenly fell sick and died. When I went to see the poor husband, he was very distressed. "Alas," he cried, "I have only one hour to live. Today according to the custom of our country, I must be buried alive beside my dead wife!"

'This, I learned, was the law, and everyone had to obey it. When the funeral preparations were finished, the procession left for the mountains, with the husband following behind. The couple were then buried together in a cave, and the husband given bread and water.

'I was so disgusted by this custom, that I told the king how I felt.

' "It is the law Sindbad, and even I must obey it if my Queen dies first."

' "Would I, a stranger to the island have to obey it?" I asked, trembling.

' "Certainly, for you have married one of us," the king answered.

'You can imagine my feelings when my own wife died a few days later! I was miserable at the thought of my fate, and although I begged for my life, it was no use.

'I was buried beside my wife in a cave, with bread and water, on which I lived for some days. When it was finished I thought there was no hope of escape. But, when I was exploring the cave I came to a tunnel. Very weak, I crawled along it and saw a small speck of light ahead. It was a narrow crack in the rock! I squeezed through this and escaped out onto the beach. I plucked up courage and went back to the cave to collect the

Sindbad made a leather saddle embroidered with gold, and some stirrups.

Sindbad ran to the ship, shouting loudly to attract the captain.

jewels and treasure that had been buried with my dear wife, and carried these to the shore.

'Two days later I saw a ship, and ran towards it, trying to attract the attention of the captain. After several attempts he spotted me and sent a boat to pick me up. Soon I was sailing back to safety and Baghdad with my treasure.

'It was not long before I desired to put to sea again. I built my own ship this time, and set sail with a rich cargo.

'We called at many islands to sell our merchandise and then stopped at an island covered in thick vegetation. We dropped anchor in one of the bays and went ashore. There we found the egg of a roc, as large as the one I had seen on my second voyage. It was almost hatched, for the baby bird had pierced the shell with its beak. When I saw my companions trying to break open the egg, I ran to stop them. I remembered the terrifying roc I had seen before and how angry the fierce bird would be when it discovered its young had been killed. I warned them of the terrible danger this could lead to but they did not listen. They cracked open the shell and roasted the young roc for supper.

'Scarcely had they finished eating the bird when the sky darkened and two immense clouds appeared in the distance. Our captain knew from experience what this was and shouted to us that the father and mother of the young roc were coming to attack us. He warned us to make for the ship quickly. This we did and set sail at once!

'The two large rocs flew towards the island uttering the most frightening cries, which grew even more terrifying when they discovered the egg was broken and their young one dead. Then they flew away towards the mountains and out of sight. We thought we had seen the last of them.

'All at once, however, the birds returned with deafening cries, both carrying huge rocks in each claw. They flew until they were exactly above our small ship and then hurled the boulders down, smashing the boat to pieces. Terrified, we all jumped into the sea, but I was the only one who was not either crushed to death or drowned.

'When I came to the surface I held onto a piece of floating wood and managed to reach yet another island. I rested for a while on the beach, amazed at my lucky escape, and went off to look for some fruit. Thus I reached a small river where an old man was sitting on the ground. When I asked him who he was, he made signs for me to carry him on my shoulders and take him across the river to the other side. This I did, but when we reached the bank he refused to get down, much to my annoyance.

'For days I had to give him food and water, and even when I was asleep he still clung to my neck. All my attempts to remove him from my shoulders were useless. One day, however, I found some gourds on the ground. I

They found the egg of a roc. It was almost hatched, for the young bird had pierced the thick shell with its beak. Sindbad warned them to stop as something terrible would happen.

scraped out their centres and made wine in them from the juice of some grapes I had picked. When I drank some, I grew so light-headed that I began to dance and sing. The old man was curious to taste some too. He liked it so much that he drank it all. The wine had the same effect on him and he began to sway to and fro on my shoulders and soon his grip loosened and I threw him to the ground. I quickly ran off.

'When I reached the shore, I found a ship anchored in the bay. The crew were astonished to see me and hear my story.

' "That was the Old Man of the Sea," they told me. "He strangles all his captives sooner or later. You are the first lucky one to escape!"

'Then we sailed off to another island famed for its coconuts. Each day we went off to one of the large forests to gather some. As the trunks of the coconut palms were so smooth, it was impossible for any one to climb them except the monkeys who lived in their thick branches. To get the nuts down, we each collected some pebbles and threw them at the monkeys. Annoyed

The birds returned carrying huge rocks which they dropped on Sindbad's boat.

by these, the monkeys would then climb to the highest branches and hurl a coconut back down at us. In this way, we soon collected quite a pile. By selling the coconuts to merchants in the city I made a considerable fortune.

'I then sailed to another island famed for its pearl fishing. Here I used divers to gather many magnificent pearls and with these and the money I had made, I sailed for home.

'About a year later I again set off for the sixth time with a captain who planned to make a long voyage. It was indeed the longest one I made. We lost our way in a storm, and had no idea where we were! When the captain eventually realised our position he was so overcome with grief that he threw his turban on the deck and tore at his beard in alarm.

'"We are in the greatest danger! A strong current is dragging the ship along and we shall all soon be drowned!"

'Then with a terrible crash, our ship was dashed against a cliff. It was split in two and destroyed, although we saved

The old man on Sindbad's shoulder liked the wine so much that he drank it all.

some of our valuable cargo.

'The mountain against which our ship had been tossed filled one side of a long island. It was so steep that there was no hope of climbing up it. The coast was covered with the wreckage of other unlucky ships like our own, and bales of valuable cargo that had been washed ashore lay everywhere. The heaps of human bones which we saw made us immediately realise that we were doomed to die. One by one my companions died. When I had buried the last of them you can imagine my despair.

'I tried to cheer myself up by exploring the island. I noticed a strange thing—a large river of fresh water ran from the sea and then disappeared into a huge deep cave in the mountain, the walls of which were covered in diamonds, rubies and other precious stones. If this river flowed underground, then it had to flow out again. I decided to build myself a raft and let the current carry me along the river. If I stayed, I would die anyway so I had nothing to lose. Perhaps the river would carry me to safety!

When the monkeys were annoyed they threw down loads and loads of coconuts.

Sindbad found parts of the wreck and made a raft.

'During that night I pondered on my escape along this roaring river. What, I thought to myself, if the river plunged into the very bowels of the earth from which there could be no possibility of escape? Again, what if the river sent me hurling over a mighty water-fall where I and my frail raft would be broken into a thousand pieces?

'All night long my thoughts could only see the bleakest end to my adventure.

'With the coming of daylight I wondered about the giant roc birds. Did they come to this island, and if they did when, and could I make my escape as I had done before?

'As the day wore on I made up my mind to explore the island just once more for a way of escape. If there were no other, then I would have to explore the river.

'I searched every nook and cranny of that strange island, but nothing— and certainly no signs of the roc birds.

'That night I slept soundly, the first time since I had been on the island. Now to my adventure.

The ship was dragged by the strong current towards the cliffs.

'I set to work at once, excitedly building my raft. I used the smashed pieces of timber from our poor ship and bound them together with rope I found on the shore. I was so eager to try and escape that this did not take me long. When all was ready I took all the rubies, emeralds and diamonds from our cargo and placed them on the raft. Having tied them down securely, I set off along the river.

'The current carried me through dark tunnels for what seemed like days. I must have fallen asleep, for the next thing I knew everything was light. I had been carried into open country and cannot describe my excitement. The raft floated on past the river banks in the sunlight. Suddenly I heard the roaring of water ahead of me and guessed that I was fast approaching a huge waterfall. I had no idea how steep it was, but realised that both the raft and myself would be ripped to pieces. Fortunately, Allah took pity on me, for I heard shouting from the bank and saw two fishermen waving to me. They hurriedly cast their nets in front of the raft and caught it just in time.

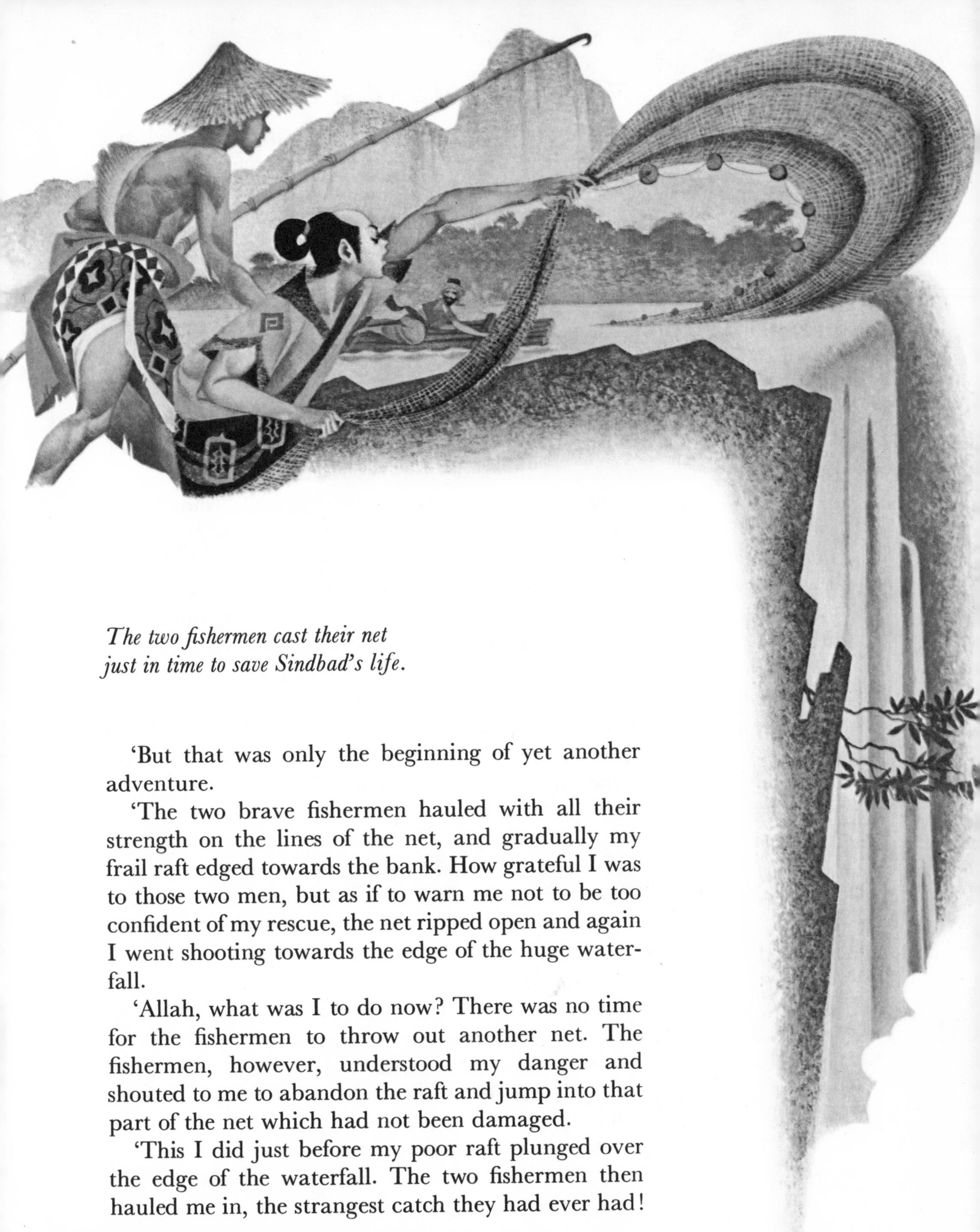

The two fishermen cast their net just in time to save Sindbad's life.

'But that was only the beginning of yet another adventure.

'The two brave fishermen hauled with all their strength on the lines of the net, and gradually my frail raft edged towards the bank. How grateful I was to those two men, but as if to warn me not to be too confident of my rescue, the net ripped open and again I went shooting towards the edge of the huge waterfall.

'Allah, what was I to do now? There was no time for the fishermen to throw out another net. The fishermen, however, understood my danger and shouted to me to abandon the raft and jump into that part of the net which had not been damaged.

'This I did just before my poor raft plunged over the edge of the waterfall. The two fishermen then hauled me in, the strangest catch they had ever had!

'I was so relieved at my escape that tears ran down my cheeks when I thanked them. They listened to my adventure in amazement and found it so wonderful they begged me to tell it to their king. I agreed to do as they wished and a few days later one of them led me to their city called Serendib to see him.

'When I reached the palace, the king received me with great kindness. He seated me by his side and asked my name. When I said I was Sindbad the Sailor and had made many voyages, he begged me to tell him about them and so I began. I told him all my adventures, and he listened eagerly.

' "I am so delighted with the story of your adventures," he declared when I had finished, "that I order that they be printed in gold letters on parchment so that I can keep them for ever."

'I then showed him my little raft and the treasures I had brought with me. I noticed how he admired the rubies and emeralds, for he had never seen such magnificent ones. When I offered them to him as a gift, he was very pleased, but refused to take my riches from me after I had faced so many dangers. He then gave me clothes and servants and built me a beautiful house. He sent me gold vases and goblets to put in it and I lived in this state of luxury for many months, in this beautiful city.

'I went regularly to his court, and entertained all his guests with the stories of my adventures. The king and I became great friends, and I was always grateful to him for his kindness. Gradually I met all the rich people in the city. This was the only place, other than Baghdad, where I was really very happy. I came to love the island and its people as if it was my own home.

'The island reminded me of paradise. I used to spend days wandering about admiring its charm and beauty. It was not large, and Serendib was situated at the end of a beautiful valley, at the foot of one of the highest mountains in the world. All kinds of lovely plants grew there.

'Having lived most of my life until now voyaging around the world I had had no time to dwell on the beauties of the living world. Only on Serendib did I have the time and the inclination to look carefully at beautiful flowers and birds and wonder at the works of Allah. In truth it was on this enchanting island that I truly learnt to love nature and understand the beautiful world I was privileged to live in.

'One day, however, I begged the king to allow me to return to my own country. Although deeply saddened, he agreed and gave me many jewels and much gold to take with me. Before I left, he asked me to deliver a letter and gifts to Caliph Haroun-al-Rashid on my return, as a token of his esteem.

'During my last few days on the island I visited the many places I had come to love so much, for I was certain that I should never see them again. Often I wondered whether I was being wise in returning to my own country. Would I ever again know the peace and beauty I had experienced on this paradise of an island?

'As much as I loved this island paradise I knew in my heart that I had to return to my own home.

'The king and I had long conversations, mostly, I have to say, about trying to persuade me to stay. He was also most interested in the ways of life in Baghdad, especially of its Great Caliph who he admired so much that he insisted in my taking back with me loads of gifts.

'What wonderful gifts he sent! Firstly, a young female slave of great beauty, dressed in the purest silk. Secondly a vase made out of one single ruby which had been cut to form a cup six inches high and one inch thick. It was filled with fine round pearls, the

The king gave me many jewels and much gold to take with me.

most perfect I have ever seen. Next, the skin of a serpent which protected anyone who lay on it from all disease. To add to this, he sent the Caliph fifty thousand gold coins and pieces of camphor as large as almond nuts. Then there were chests of gold and silver, jewelled vases, rolls of exquisite silks and fine brocades. There were beautiful carpets for the Caliph's palace, and richly embroidered tapestries to hang on the walls. Finally, there were priceless jewelled rings and daggers of great beauty.

'The next morning he gave me one of his own fine ships and men of his own crew to sail me safely home. There was so much for me to take back with me, that it took a whole morning to load everything on board. It was with great sorrow that the king and I said goodbye.

'After a long journey we arrived safely at the port of Balsura and travelled to Baghdad. I immediately delivered the letter and gifts to the Caliph Haroun-al-Rashid, and presented the slave to him. The Caliph had never seen such magnificent pearls or rubies. I told him of everything that had happened on the island and how the king and I were great friends. The Caliph was delighted and rewarded me handsomely!

'After my sixth voyage I decided never to go to sea again. I was now getting old and needed a life of ease and rest. I had travelled enough and made my fortune. What is more, I was afraid of any further dangers I might meet if I did set sail once more.

'One day, however, when I was dining with some friends I received an urgent message to go and see the Caliph. I was rather surprised but obeyed at once.

' "Sindbad," said the Caliph, "I want you to do me a favour. You must go once more to the King of Serendib with my answer and gifts. It is only polite that I should return his generosity."

' "Your Majesty, I am your loyal servant and ready to do whatever you command me," I said. "But I beg you to remember that I am already wearied by six hard long voyages and all the dangers that I have had to face. I have sworn never to leave Baghdad again!"

'I then told him of all my adventures, and he listened with interest.

' "Your adventures are indeed extraordinary, Sindbad," he said, "but you must do what I ask. The island of Serendib is not all that far away, and when you have done this small favour, you will be free to live a peaceful and restful life."

'I saw that the Caliph had made up his mind and that I could not refuse his wishes. I prepared a ship for my departure and set off for the island of Serendib with the Caliph's letter and gifts for the King. There

The king gave gifts to the Great Caliph. Firstly, a young female slave of great beauty, dressed in pure silk.

were beautiful rich brocades and fine linen, a bed of gold, jewelled vases, marble statues and richly decorated tables said to have once belonged to King Solomon!

'We had been at sea for several days when we sailed into a thick mist, and could not see to steer our vessel. When I was beginning to think we were lost, one of the crew spotted land and I soon saw the tall mountains of the island of Serendib rising up in the distance.

'How mistaken I was! The tall mountains grew taller as we approached them, but we could see no harbour. Suddenly the tall mountains disappeared as the sky was ripped by a tongue of fork lightning and a roll of thunder which shook the very timbers of the ship. The sea which until that moment had been as calm as a pool was now lashing and rolling.

'The captain of the vessel and his crew hauled in the sails and roped down everything on deck. The captain ordered me to my quarters, telling me to tie myself to a stout timber in case the ship broke its back.

'As we were tossed about like a cork I had fears that I was about to set out on yet another adventure, and perhaps one from which I would never return. I must say my heart was sad, especially as I would never again see my beloved Serendib.

'For twenty-four hours the storm tossed the vessel about so much that I was certain that it could no longer resist the forces of the storm. But my prayers to Allah were answered for as suddenly as it had sprung up, so the storm dropped. The sea was again like a pool, but what is more we were facing the harbour of Serendib.

'The captain wasted no time in hoisting the sails and piloting his ship into the safety of the harbour. How happy was I to put my feet on dry land.

'Having landed, I quickly made for the palace, and asked to see the King. A few minutes later he greeted me.

' "Why Sindbad! My dear friend, what a pleasure to see you. I thought I would never see you again. Come, let us feast and drink to celebrate your arrival!"

'When we had eaten I gave him the Caliph's gifts and letters.

' "Tell your Caliph that he is most kind to show his friendship by sending such magnificent gifts," he said with pleasure and bade me farewell.

Sindbad returned to his beloved Baghdad to live in peace and quiet.

'After three or four days at sea, we were attacked by pirates who easily captured our ship and treasure, as we had few weapons with which to defend ourselves. We were then taken to a distant island where the pirates sold us for slaves!

'I had the good fortune to be bought by a rich merchant who took me to his home. He treated me well, and I became his servant. As the island where he lived was not too far from Baghdad, I sold a ring that the King of Serendib had given me and which the pirates had not seen. With the money, I bought myself some new clothes and paid the fare back to my country. A few days later I arrived in Baghdad, having escaped to freedom once more! I would now be able to live the quiet life I had longed for after so many weary years on the Seas.'

And so Sindbad ended the story of his most exciting and adventurous voyages. Then turning to Hindbad, he said:

"Well, my friend, have you ever heard of anybody who has been in as many and such terrible dangers as I? Do I not deserve to have an easy restful life after having suffered so much?"

"I must agree," replied Hindbad, as he knelt down before his host. "Compared with what you have told me I have suffered very little and faced few dangers. It is indeed just that you should now lead the life you do. You are worthy of all the riches you own, and I was so unjust to you, but it was jealousy—a terrible sin. Please forgive me, as I hope Allah will."

"You speak wisely," Sindbad said. "Here, my good fellow, take this bag of gold as a gift, and let us be friends. Feel free to come and visit me whenever you wish."

"You are kind to treat me so," replied Hindbad. "May you live happily to the end of your days."

Saleh the Merchant

Saleh was a merchant and lived in the famous city of Baghdad. His father had been a corn-dealer by trade and over the years had amassed a large sum of money which he left to Saleh, who, for a time, carried on this profitable business.

Saleh had an ambition to become still richer, and so he decided to journey to the city of Shiraz in Persia. A friend had told him that there was a lot of money to be made there.

"Listen to me, Saleh," he said. "In Shiraz sandal-wood is very scarce and will fetch an excellent price! That is what you must sell, if you want to become wealthy."

So Saleh sold all the corn in his warehouse and with the money he received he bought up every piece of

sandal-wood he could find. He hired some of the thirty camels he possessed to the camel merchants in Baghdad. Then, having loaded up the rest with his precious store of wood, he started on the long journey to the distant city of Shiraz, dreaming of the fortune he would surely make.

He travelled for days on foot in the intense heat, and grew very weary. And then one day he caught sight of the minarets of a mosque and the gleaming gold domes of the city in the distance. Excitedly he hurried towards the city walls. On the way he met an old shepherdess tending her sheep by the roadside.

"What brings you to our city, stranger?" she asked.

"I am a merchant from Baghdad, and

As Saleh hurried excitedly towards the city walls he met an old shepherdess tending her sheep by the roadside, and she asked him what brought him to her city.

have come to make my fortune here in Shiraz," Saleh replied.

"Beware young man!" the old woman said. "Let me warn you about the dangers of this city. You are a stranger here and Shiraz is full of thieves and cheats who will rob you of all you have, if you are not careful. If you want to remain safe do not tell anyone you have just arrived in the city!"

Saleh thanked the old woman for her advice, but paid little attention to her warning.

"I am not as foolish as she obviously thinks I am!" he said to himself. "As if anyone could cheat ME!"

By the time Saleh entered the city, night had already fallen and it was very dark and quiet. The first thing to do was to find somewhere to stay. He found an inn, tied up his camels, and stumbled into bed exhausted. The next morning he awoke early, and after breakfast asked the way to the market-place.

In the market a man whom Saleh took to be a merchant spoke to him.

"Welcome! I see from your

Saleh entered Shiraz when night had already fallen. The first thing he had to do was find somewhere to stay.

clothes that you are a stranger in Shiraz. Why have you come to our city?"

"I have travelled here from Baghdad to sell my merchandise," Saleh answered.

"And what merchandise have you brought with you?"

"I have a large supply of sandal-wood to sell. I believe it will fetch a very high price here," replied Saleh.

Saleh is asked why he had come to Shiraz.

"Who on earth told you that!" replied the man. "It is not true at all. Here, sandal-wood is worth no more than the drift wood we collect on the river bank. It is hardly worth anything, and only fit for lighting fires to cook on!"

"What am I to do?" Saleh asked despairingly. "I am ruined!"

"I have an idea," said the man—who was really a thief and had lied about the value of the sandal-wood. "My friend, I will buy your worthless sandal-wood for one piece of gold. That is a very generous price."

"It is not enough," Saleh replied. "I spent most of my fortune buying the sandal-wood. It must be worth more!"

"Don't be foolish, young man," the thief said, beginning to get angry. "Who else would offer you more for what is nothing more than kindlings for the cooking fire? Never look a gift horse in the mouth. Besides, I may be able to help you. I have many friends in Shiraz who will be pleased to give you work."

Saleh was so grateful for this offer that he agreed.

Thrilled at the success of his trick, the thief hurried off with the valuable load of sandal-wood which had only cost him one piece of gold, knowing he could sell it for almost twenty times as much! After hiding the wood until he could sell it profitably, he lit a fire with some ordinary logs, and cooked supper for himself and another thief, to whom he told the story.

"I bet the stranger is angry, Houssain," his friend said, chuckling with glee. "How clever of you to make him believe all that sandal-wood was worth nothing!"

"It is so easy to trick these strangers who come into the city," Houssain replied. "They make perfect victims! Let us tell our leader and try and sell the wood tomorrow."

Poor Saleh, meanwhile, sat on the pavement with his head in his hands. He had exchanged his precious merchandise for just one gold coin!

"I still have the money the camel merchants gave me to hire my animals. I shan't allow myself to be tricked again!"

The morning after this unfortunate incident, Saleh again went to the market, the old woman's warning ringing in his ears.

As he was walking past one of the stalls, someone suddenly grabbed his arm! Spinning round with fright, he saw the horrible face of a beggar, with a patch over one eye, staring at him evilly.

"Stop thief! Stop thief!" the beggar shouted, "at last I have caught you! It was you who made me blind many years ago, and stole all my money!"

"What are you talking about," Saleh stammered in astonishment.

The thief lit a fire with some ordinary logs, and cooked supper for himself and another thief to whom he told the story of how he had bought the sandalwood for one piece of gold.

"I have never seen you before in my life. I only arrived here from Baghdad last night!"

But the beggar only shouted louder, and gripped his arm more tightly. By this time a huge crowd had gathered and poor Saleh grew frightened. What he did not know was that this was a cunning trick the beggar and his friends always played on rich-looking strangers to obtain their money. Presently one of the beggar's friends spoke.

"Now, be quiet and let us settle this matter! If what you say is true, then this thief must pay you enough money to make up for such a crime!"

Saleh could not prove his innocence, and had to part with almost all the money he had.

Trembling from this dreadful experience, Saleh went back to the inn for his mid-day meal. On returning to the market-place he noticed that the soles of his shoes were worn. As there was a cobbler's shop nearby, he asked the cobbler to repair them.

"Certainly Sir," the cobbler replied. "It will cost you three pieces of gold!"

Saleh thought this very expensive, but he paid.

Shortly afterwards, he saw the old shepherdess again, sitting on a stone. Saleh told her his tale of woe about the sandal-wood and how the beggar had also tricked him.

The old woman listened patiently to his story. "I wish to help you, young man," she said. "Just outside the city is the house of a rich merchant. This man is the leader of all the robbers in the city. Go there and find out

The beggar shouted louder, and gripped his arm more tightly. By this time a crowd had gathered to watch what was happening, and poor Saleh grew frightened.

what the thieves are planning to do next. With luck you will be able to get back some of the money you lost."

Saleh thanked the old woman for her kind advice and made straight for the place she had described to him—where he saw the leader of the robbers sitting on a mat in front of a large rock. Saleh crept behind this rock without being seen. He had not been there long, when to his surprise, he saw the two scoundrels who had tricked him! They greeted their leader respectfully and sat down cross-legged on the ground in front of him.

Saleh watched everything in astonished silence. There sat the merchant who had tricked him into believing his stock of wood was worthless! Beside him was the one-eyed man who had cunningly obtained his money by means of an evil lie. Then, to his amazement, the cobbler who had repaired his shoes also arrived.

"Let me hear what success you have had today," the robbers' leader asked.

It was the merchant's turn to speak first. "Yesterday afternoon I came across a stranger who had travelled all the way from Baghdad with a precious load of sandal-wood, intending to sell it

The cobbler repaired Saleh's shoes as the soles were very worn.

here and make a huge profit. I persuaded him that the wood was worth nothing. This upset him so much that, without stopping to think, he sold it all to me for one piece of gold! I have now sold the wood for twenty times as much! Was I not extremely clever?"

"You did very well," replied the leader. "Has anyone else something interesting to tell me?"

"Yes!" replied the one-eyed beggar. "This morning I met a stranger in the market square. He was so well dressed that I guessed he must have a fat purse of gold on him, so I seized his arm and accused him of having blinded and robbed me many years ago. I made so much fuss that a crowd of my friends gathered round us. We demanded that unless he paid for his awful crime straight away we would throw him in prison. There was

The shepherdess tells Saleh that he has been tricked by the leader of all the robbers in Shiraz.

no way the poor fellow could prove his innocence, so he had to pay up! He was so terrified, it was really very funny. Was I not very shrewd and clever?"

"You have done well, blind man," replied his master.

Then came the cobbler's turn to speak. Saleh was interested to learn what he had done to please his master.

"A few hours ago, master, a stranger came into my shop. The soles of his shoes were worn, and he asked me to repair them. As he was finely dressed, I realised he was probably quite rich, so I charged him far more than he should have paid, in fact three times as much. When he commented on how expensive this was, I explained that I charged a high price because I was the best cobbler in all of Shiraz."

"You are learning, cobbler," his master replied. "You have not earned as much as your other two friends, but then you are new to this game. Well done!"

The fifth member of the group was an innkeeper who reported that he had overcharged all the

The cobbler told how he had repaired the shoes of the stranger and charged him three times more than he should.

visitors to his inn.

Saleh was stunned with amazement at all he had overheard. "Everyone in the city must be in league with each other, trying to trick as many strangers as they can! I must make my fortune as quickly as possible and then leave before I am cheated again!" he thought.

"Innkeeper," the thieves' leader commanded, "go quickly to our secret cave in the mountains, and see that all we have stored there is safe!

These three strangers will be so furious, that if they ever discovered it and found it belonged to us, they would surely rob us of everything in it!"

"I will go at once," said the innkeeper.

"You, cobbler," ordered the master thief, "get back to the market-place, and find some more fools like the merchant from Baghdad."

"Yes, master," replied the cobbler, and scurried off to do as he had been ordered.

"As for you, merchant," the master thief said, "see if you can buy another load of sandal-wood for one gold piece. Better still, see if you can buy a load of silk for the price of cotton."

"Yes, master," replied the merchant, and he too scurried off to do as he had been ordered.

On hearing this, Saleh pricked up his ears. What a stroke of luck! He decided to follow the innkeeper and get him to lead him straight to the cave. In order to avenge himself, he would rob the thieves of their own stolen riches!

"No one could accuse me of being dishonest," he thought. "For after all I am only recovering what is rightfully mine, and perhaps a little more besides, to pay these rogues back for their treachery!"

Saleh crept out of the garden and followed the innkeeper at a safe distance.

They came to a wide valley, whose entrance was so narrow that it was difficult to pass through. Once beyond it, they reached a remarkably steep mountain. Saleh watched the innkeeper start to climb up it. As Saleh looked, he saw the innkeeper push open and enter a huge stone door in the mountain.

"That must be the cave," he said to himself, excitedly. "I shall wait until the innkeeper leaves and then climb up and go inside to have a look for myself!"

Saleh waited patiently. After about half an hour the innkeeper came out and hurried back to tell his master that everything was in order. This was the chance Saleh had been waiting for. Quickly, he climbed up to the stone door and pushed it open. He went down some steps, and came to a deep, rather dark cave. Before him he saw row upon row of sacks, brimming with gold and gems.

He decided to return the next day with his camels.

Saleh hurried off back to his inn in Shiraz to prepare for his departure. He went to bed early, dreaming of his good fortune.

The next morning, before anyone else in the city was awake, he hurried off with his camels to the cave. He carried sack after sack of gold and gems down to his camels, and having loaded them up, set off on his long journey home.

As Saleh was leading his camels along the road he met the shepherdess who had greeted him when he first entered the city.

"You have not stayed in our city very long," said the shepherdess.

"No," Saleh replied. "I took your advice and went to the house of the rich merchant. There I overheard their plans, and how I had been robbed."

"Did you get your sandal-wood back?" asked the shepherdess.

"I got more than my sandal-wood back," replied Saleh.

"How was that possible?" the shepherdess asked.

"Well," replied Saleh, "the thieves hide their stolen gold and jewels in a cave, and I followed the innkeeper who had been ordered to make sure that their treasure was safe. My camels now carry the thieves' riches!"

The innkeeper hurried off to see that the treasure was safe.

"Good for you, young merchant," said the shepherdess. "Those scoundrels deserve to be taught a lesson."

"Before I go on my way," Saleh said, "I would like to make you a present of this bag of gold. Since I arrived in Shiraz you are the only person who has helped me; in fact, if it were not for you I should be begging in the market-place."

"Thank you, young merchant," the old woman replied. "Remember that not all the people of Shiraz are robbers and thieves. Many kind and honest people abide here."

Saleh bowed to the shepherdess, mounted his lead-camel and set off with his precious riches.

In this way, Saleh returned to Baghdad a wealthy man. He had learned his lesson and made sure that no-one ever cheated him again.

Saleh loaded his camels with sack after sack of gold and gems, and returned to Baghdad a wealthy man.

Abu Sir and Abu Kir

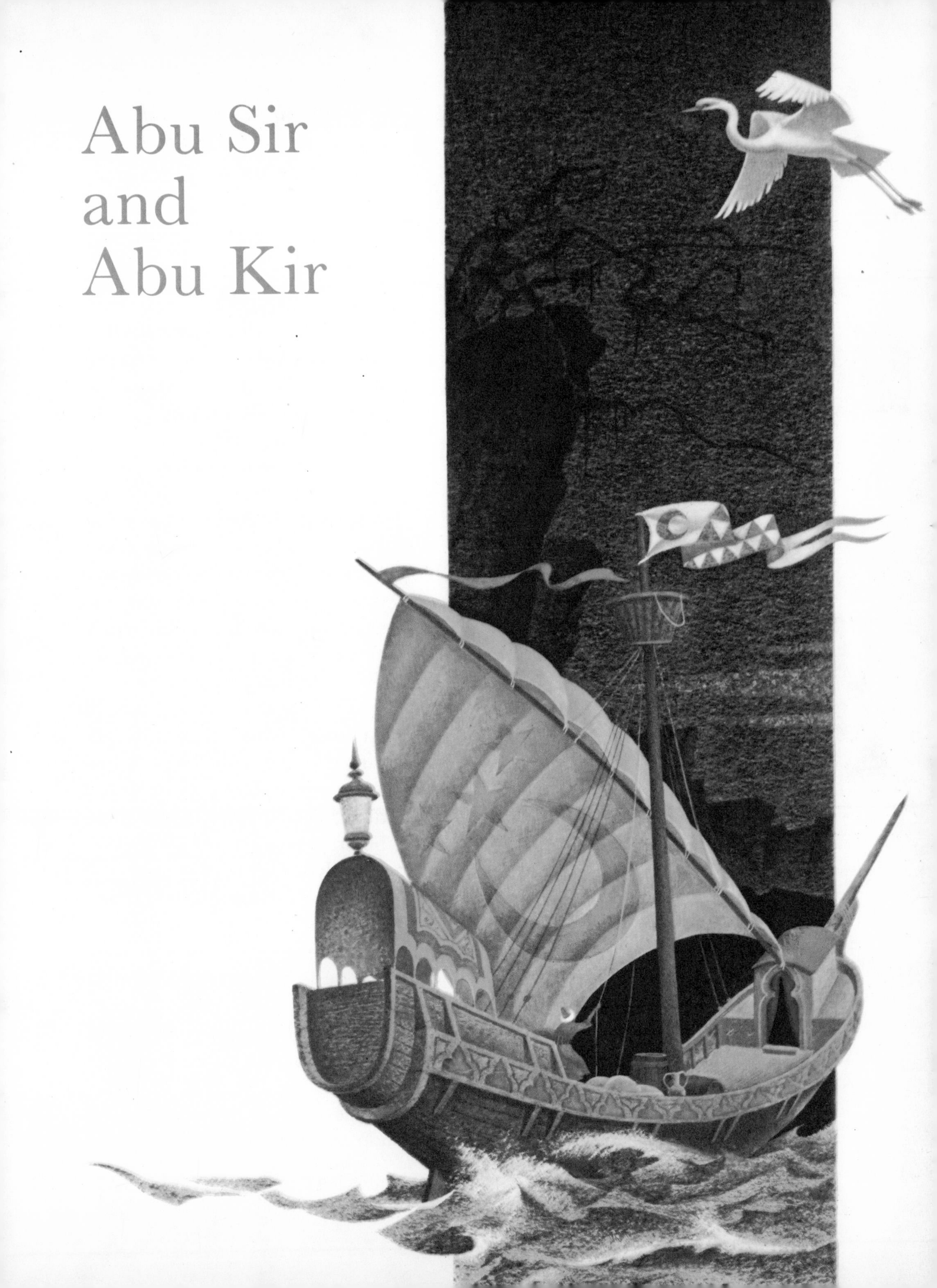

Abu Sir was a very kind young man who, though poor, never did a dishonest thing.

There were once two men who lived in Alexandria. One, Abu Kir, was a dyer, and his shop was next to that of the other, Abù Sir, a barber.

Although their names were similar, their characters were very different. Abu Sir was a very kind and considerate young man, who although very poor, never did a dishonest or unkind thing. His neighbour was the exact opposite! Abu Kir was a cheat and a liar. He was so dishonest that he always insisted on his customers paying him in advance, when they brought him cloth to dye. Then, when they came to collect it, he would deny ever having seen them before, and then sell their cloth secretly for his own profit.

One day he did just this to a rich merchant, who had brought him many bales of cloth to dye two weeks before.

"Why, you rogue," the merchant shouted, "you remember me very well. I brought you in twenty rolls of cloth to have dyed and even paid in advance! Where are they, you cheat!"

The merchant grew so angry that his shouts could be heard at the end of the street, and in threatening to hit Abu Kir he upset all his bowls of dye onto the floor.

For a long time Abu Kir managed to earn a good living by such deceitful ways, but eventually no-one went to his shop any more.

In threatening to hit Abu Kir, the angry merchant upset all the bowls of dye onto the floor.

Realising he was a ruined man, Abu Kir went and sat outside the barber's shop. When Abu Sir came out and saw him, the dyer said sadly:

"Alas! I shall soon starve to death. I have no money to buy food. No one comes to my shop any more!"

The barber felt sorry for him. "Listen! I shall help you," he said. "Come and stay with me and eat and drink here."

Abu Kir immediately agreed to the barber's kind offer, out of selfishness, and not gratitude.

There he lived for a long time, with Abu Sir supplying all his needs. One day Abu Sir said how difficult he found it to earn a decent living.

"Oh, Abu Kir, no-one can say that I am not a good barber. I do my work well and my hand is light. I never overcharge and always give my customers value for money. But because my shop is shabby and I am so poor, only a rare sailor or a porter comes here to be shaved, so I only earn a few coppers."

"I cannot understand," said Abu Kir irritably, "how you can put up with these hardships so patiently, when you have no hope of becoming rich and living in luxury. Your trade fails and my business fails, all because of the meanness of our fellow citizens! If they came to our shops we would each have a thriving business, and make a decent living."

"But what can we do?" asked Abu Sir in despair.

"The only thing for us is to leave this cruel city and country of ours and travel to a place where both our trades are properly appreciated! Travelling is so marvellous, you know, Abu Sir—lots of fresh air, seeing new lands and cities, and a chance to practise trades honoured throughout the world, such as yours and mine!"

"Well let us set off at once to make our fortunes!" exclaimed Abu Sir excitedly.

So he hurriedly packed up basins, razors, scissors, combs, brushes and irons and they both headed down to the harbour. What luck! A vessel was being loaded by the crew and about to set sail! They quickly went on board.

Fortunately, fate was with them during the voyage, for out of the other hundred and forty passengers on board, there was no other barber but Abu Sir! When the ship had been at sea for several days, Abu Sir said to the dyer.

"Abu Kir, we have no food or

Abu Sir and Abu Kir set off hurriedly and found a vessel about to set sail.

drink. I shall go round the passengers and sailors, offering them my services as a barber, in case anyone should wish me to shave him. That way I can earn food, or water or money."

"What an excellent idea," exclaimed the lazy dyer. "But listen! Do you agree that, as we are helping each other, each of us should put his profits into a fund which we shall divide when we return to Alexandria? We must also agree that whoever finds work, should provide for the other."

"Oh yes," said Abu Sir, "after all, that is only fair."

"Go and earn some money then," snapped Abu Kir as he made himself comfortable on the deck and prepared to go to sleep.

With his razor, bowl and towel, Abu Sir walked amongst the passengers and sailors to see who wanted a shave. He shaved one passenger for two rolls, another for a piece of cheese, another for a basket of olives, one more for a slice of water melon, another for a few coppers, and another for some buns.

The sailors and passengers found Abu Sir so kind and pleasant that they felt very sorry for him. Abu Sir became so popular that news of him even reached the ears of the ship's captain.

"Send this young barber to me," the captain ordered, "so he can shave me as well. I am anxious to meet such a popular man!"

Abu Sir entered the captain's cabin and began to shave him. During the course of their conversation the barber could not help mentioning how great the misery of poverty was, and that he had a travelling companion to support. The captain was a kind man too, and liked Abu Sir, whose charming manners and kind nature delighted him.

"Why don't you and your friend come and have dinner with me every evening until the end of this voyage? It would give me a great deal of pleasure to have you as my guests."

Abu Sir was so grateful to the captain for such great generosity that, having thanked him warmly, he rushed back to tell Abu Kir the good news.

"I feel seasick and cannot go," growled Abu Kir. "You go and dine with the captain. I am so ill!"

That evening, therefore, Abu Sir went alone to dine with the captain, and feasted off a table spread with twenty or more dishes of delicious, mouth-watering food.

For the rest of the voyage Abu Sir spent his time in shaving the passengers and sailors and dining with the captain, whilst the idle Abu Kir did nothing but sleep and eat the food which the barber earned.

They lived like this for twenty days and on the twenty-first day the ship docked in the harbour of a foreign city.

The barber and the dyer gathered together their belongings, and having said goodbye to the captain, went ashore. They spent all that afternoon looking for somewhere to stay, before they found an inn where they rented a room.

As Abu Kir said he still felt seasick, the barber left him asleep and took all his razors, basins, brushes and towels into the city where he offered his services as a barber.

At first, only porters or street-sellers gave him business, but soon all the well-to-do merchants heard of his skill, and became his customers.

Abu Sir spent his time shaving passengers and sailors.

Gradually, Abu Sir made a lot of money, and each evening he would return with food for himself and his lazy companion. It was only because Abu Sir was so very kind and considerate that he did not realise how much the rascal Abu Kir was making use of him. Abu Kir did not lift a finger to help.

Every evening he would greedily eat the delicious food Abu Sir had brought, and then go off to sleep. Even after forty days, he still pretended to be seasick, so that Abu Sir would do all the work, and all this time the good barber never once complained about his friend's conduct.

One day, however, Abu Sir fell ill himself and could no longer go out to work. He became so weak that he lost consciousness and lay very still. This annoyed the unsympathetic dyer, for he was hungry and there was no food to eat, except for some scraps. So, he was forced to get up and go to buy some.

One morning when Abu Sir was fast asleep the ungrateful Abu Kir

The idle Abu Kir would eat the delicious foods and then go off to sleep.

searched through the barber's clothes and found his purse, which contained all the money he had saved. Abu Kir grabbed it eagerly, and without giving his sick friend another thought—despite all Abu Sir had done for him—crept out of the room and shut the door. He quickly tiptoed out of the garden and made for the city.

Poor Abu Sir was therefore left completely helpless, and never suspected for a moment what the wicked dyer had done, for he was too ill! All the money he had so carefully saved, the treacherous dyer had taken with him.

The first thing the dyer did was to make for the most expensive restaurant in the city and have a huge meal. He ordered so much food that it took him a whole hour to eat it all! He never once thought about his sick, hungry friend.

Then he went off to the market, where he visited all the rich merchants and eagerly examined what they had to sell. He bought himself a

magnificent new set of clothes, and then took a walk through the streets. He was delighted by everything the city had to offer, and which he could now afford. He forgot, on purpose, that the money he had to spend was not his at all!

One thing, however, struck him as very strange. All the inhabitants of the city were dressed either in white or blue! The shops sold nothing but white or blue merchandise. Everything around him was white or blue! He wondered what the reason was! The greatest surprise came when he went into a dyer's shop and saw that the vats only contained indigo, to dye things blue.

"Oh master of the trade," he asked, "what colour can you dye this handkerchief for me?"

"Blue, Sir," replied the dyer.

"But what if I want it red?"

"Then that is impossible, sir. There is no such thing as a red dye."

"Then dye it green, or yellow!" replied Abu Kir in astonishment.

"But, Sir, I have never heard of a green or yellow dye!"

The barber and the dyer went ashore and found an inn where they rented a room.

shouted the dyer. "What you ask is quite impossible!"

When Abu Kir recited all the shades of dye that he knew, he saw that the man did not understand a word he said, and so he asked if all the other dyers in the city only knew of a blue dye too.

"There are forty of us, sir, in the city," the dyer replied, "and none of us have ever heard of any other dye but a blue one!"

"Oh master of the trade, I too am a dyer by profession, and I can change materials into all the colours of the rainbow, using dyes you have never heard of! Let me work for you and I shall show you the secret of my art!"

"We are not allowed to employ strangers!" the dyer explained angrily to Abu Kir.

This was the reply from all the other dyers in the city too, and Abu Kir was so furious that he went to complain to the king.

When the king heard the range of colours Abu Kir could dye materials, he was delighted.

Abu Kir grabbed the bag containing Abu Sir's money and he crept out of the room.

Abu Kir thought it very strange that the stalls sold only white or blue materials.

"Why! If you are telling the truth and can really dye materials in all these marvellous colours, I shall build you a shop and dye factory myself, and give you all the money you need to run it!" the king promised.

Before long Abu Kir had the most magnificent dye factory and all the money he wanted. He set to work dyeing the bales of silk the king had sent him—green, yellow, red, purple, blue and every colour you can think of! He hung them outside to dry, and all the passers-by marvelled at the beauty of the colours blowing in the breeze.

At the sight of such brightly coloured silk, the King was so overjoyed and delighted that he made Abu Kir the Royal Dyer! He showered him with wealth, and from that day, Abu Kir dressed like a king himself, in magnificent gold brocades and jewelled turbans. He was at last very rich, something he had always wanted!

Soon, the streets and markets were crowded with people wearing the splendid bright colours Abu Kir had created, and there

was no blue to be seen, for everyone was so sick of it! Abu Kir became one of the most respected men in the city.

The barber, meanwhile, was no better. He had lain ill for three whole days before the innkeeper had discovered how sick he was.

"What is the matter, Abu Sir?" the innkeeper asked, seeing the barber groaning and looking so weak on his mat. "Where is your friend?"

"I do not know, innkeeper. Please give me something to drink."

Presently the innkeeper returned with a bowl of hot broth which he fed to his patient. For two months he cared for him himself. Gradually, Abu Sir's health improved until he was completely recovered.

By this time, of course, Abu Sir had discovered the loss of his purse. As he never thought ill of anyone he presumed that his friend Abu Kir must have borrowed it. He collected up all his possessions and, having thanked the innkeeper for all his kindness, left for the city.

As he was wandering through the streets, he came to Abu Kir's factory, where a great crowd had gathered to admire the colours of the materials hanging out to dry. He asked one of the bystanders why there were so many people outside.

"This is the shop of the Sultan's dyer, Abu Kir. He has invented all these colours by some secret art, and has now become very rich!"

"Thanks be to Allah that he has made his fortune!" Abu Sir thought happily. "How wrong I was to think ill of him. If he borrowed my purse it was only to buy dyes with. Now I shall see how gratefully he will welcome me, and reward me! He will rejoice at seeing me again!"

Abu Sir eventually managed to squeeze his way through the crowd, and reach the door of Abu Kir's shop. He looked inside and saw the dyer lounging in magnificence on a great throne of cushions, dressed in robes fit for a king and surrounded by slaves.

"How pleased he will be to see me," thought Abu Sir.

But as soon as their eyes met, Abu Kir went white—and shouted, "Thief! Thief! Seize him, slave!"

Immediately one of the slaves leapt at poor Abu Sir, who fell to the floor with shock, and started to beat him violently with a huge stick.

If I ever set eyes on you again," screamed the wicked Abu Kir in his fury, "I shall send you to the King and have your head cut off. Begone, you wretch, and never enter my sight again!"

After the cruel beating given him by Abu Kir, the poor barber lay in pain on his bed.

BAR.

At this, the poor barber, humiliated and in pain, and heart-broken to receive such cruelty from someone he thought was his friend, dragged himself away to the inn in tears, as the crowd hurled insults and curses at him.

When he arrived at the inn he lay on his bed all night long, in bitter grief at the dyer's evil words. He just could not understand such treachery!

"How could he be so unfriendly," he asked himself, "after all I did for him? I am his friend, not his enemy," he sobbed in despair.

The next morning he got up and felt much better. He decided to go and have a bath, but found there was nowhere for him to have one. No-one knew what he was talking about! Astonished at this, he asked a jar-seller who was walking down the street where he could have one.

"Have a bath? I do not know what that is! When we want to wash, we go and bathe in the sea! I have never heard of a special place where you go to have one."

Abu Sir could not believe that these people knew nothing about hot baths and a hammam (which in the East is the name for the building where you can go and have one) for only a few people there have a bath in their own house. He was so shocked, in fact, that he decided to go to the palace, and demand an audience with the king!

Fortunately, the king agreed to see him. He was an old, bearded man with a very dignified, yet gentle, manner. The barber kissed his hand and paying him the usual respects said,

"Your majesty, I am a stranger to your city, and a barber by trade, having come from Alexandria. Today I wished to take a bath, and visit the hammam of your city, but no-one could tell me the way to it, or even understood what the word meant. Now, a hammam is a necessity in any city, and

A slave leapt at poor Abu and beat him with a stick.

BAR.

it is simply astonishing that a beautiful city like yours does not have one."

"But what is a hammam?" asked the bewildered king.

"Why a hammam is a bath-house, a building where one goes to take a hot bath. It is the only place where one can wash properly and become really clean. Your city will never be perfect until you have one. It is an absolute necessity for the health of your citizens!" Abu Sir explained.

The king was delighted by this idea!

"Welcome to our city, oh barber," he cried, "you shall have all you wish and more. I love the sound of such a building. I shall have one built for you at once."

Before long, the King had given Abu Sir a special robe of honour, a magnificent horse, some slaves and a beautiful palace. In fact, he thought more highly of Abu Sir than he did of his Royal Dyer, and gave the barber his best architects to design the hammam.

Abu Sir toured the city, and when he had chosen a suitable spot, commanded them to build there. Following his instructions, the architects constructed the most beautiful hammam the world had ever seen. It was built of the rarest white marble, with red velvet carpets and green silk curtains draped everywhere. With the extra money Abu Sir received he bought towels of linen and silk, precious soaps and essences, and the rarest perfumes. As soon as the hammam was completely furnished and all was in order, Abu Sir told the king, and invited him to see it!

When the day for the opening arrived, Abu Sir heated the hammam and the water in the baths and turned on the fountains which decorated the interior. The spray fell so sweetly that it was like the gentle tinkling of music.

The king arrived presently, dressed in a rich robe of white brocade, and Abu Sir knelt to him respectfully as he entered.

A jar-seller told Abu Sir that the only place he could wash was at the sea.

Delighted with the idea of a bath-house the king ordered one built at once.

As soon as the king crossed the threshold of the great arch, he was amazed. His eyes could not believe the exquisite carving and magnificence of the interior. He was enchanted by the exotic perfumes he smelt and the soft music of the fountains playing all around him.

"But I have never seen anything so perfect!" he exclaimed.

"Your majesty, you must take a bath to fully appreciate the pleasures of such a place."

So the king undressed and entered the marble bath of warm rose-scented water. He washed with turtle soap, and was astonished at how relaxed and calm he became. He felt as light as a bird, and his skin was as smooth as silk.

"I have never felt so healthy and well in my life, Abu Sir!" he cried with delight. "This is truly an excellent idea to wash in such pleasant surroundings instead of the sea. My city is indeed beautiful but imperfect without such a hammam! You must build a few more, so that everyone can enjoy them!"

"Your majesty, you are too kind! But now you see the truth of what I told you, and the necessity of such a place."

"Yes, Abu Sir, you are wise and I must reward you well. Today, I shall ask my Treasurer to send you twenty sacks of gold as proof of my extreme gratitude! Meanwhile, you must build me my own private hammam at the palace."

As everyone paid to use the hammam, except the very poor, Abu Sir soon amassed quite a fortune for crowds thronged daily to try this new luxury. Every day he became richer and surrounded in more honour and glory, but still remained as modest and honest as before. He was always generous to the poor and this kindness one day saved his life, as you will see later.

Abu Kir, the dyer, naturally heard of the hammam too, and full of jealousy, decided to try it. The first person he saw was Abu Sir himself!

"Welcome," Abu Sir cried, running to greet his friend, "how good it is to see you Abu Kir. Come and take a bath, and see how you like my hammam," he said without any bitterness. "I

shall give you my best essences and creams to clean yourself with. You shall have a better bath than the king himself!" he said.

So Abu Kir entered, and all the other bathers were annoyed to see the Royal Dyer receiving such special treatment, usually only given to the king himself. When he had finished he went up to Abu Sir and said,

"Your hammam is admirable, but it lacks just one thing to make it truly marvellous," he said with an evil tone in his voice.

"What is that?" asked the unsuspecting barber, anxious to do anything to make the hammam even better.

"It is a special cream for making skin smooth. To make it you need yellow arsenic and quicklime. Mix these with a little oil and store it in a clay jar. This paste really works wonders! The king will love it when he sees his skin even smoother and whiter than all these essences can make it."

When Abu Sir had made a note of the ingredients, Abu Kir left the hammam and hurried off to see the king with his evil plan.

Abu Sir greeted the King respectfully and asked him what he thought of the bath-house.

Abu Sir ran to greet his friend Abu Kir and invited him to take a bath in his hammam.

Abu Sir, meanwhile, quickly prepared the paste, using the recipe his friend had given him, and stored it away as a surprise for the king.

At the palace, however, Abu Kir demanded to see the king.

"Your majesty," he said bowing before him, "I have come to warn you of the treachery of Abu Sir who keeps the hammam."

"But what are you talking about, Abu Kir!" asked the astonished king angrily.

"If you go to the hammam, your majesty, you will die. Abu Sir is a traitor and has been sent by your enemies to poison you, for he has prepared a cream containing yellow arsenic and quicklime. He will suggest that you rub it into your skin to make it smooth and white. But the moment you apply it, the poison will act and your flesh will burn like fire!"

As the king trusted the dyer, he naturally believed what he said and was so terrified by these lies that his admiration for the barber turned into violent hatred.

"Tell no-one of this!" he ordered, quaking with fear, "and I shall go with two slaves to the hammam at once, to see if what you say is true."

As soon as the king arrived at the bath-house, Abu Sir greeted him and led him inside to a private bath.

"Oh mighty king" said the barber with delight, "I have a surprise for you. I have found a cream which will make your skin whiter and smoother than all these other lotions I have. Here take it and rub some on!"

At this the king was fully convinced of the truth of Abu Kir's warning.

"Arrest this murderer!" he shouted as his two slaves rushed forward to grab the astonished barber.

Abu Sir was dragged off to the deepest dungeon in the Royal Palace, protesting strongly, and quite unable to understand what he could have done to make the king so angry.

He spent a very miserable, sleepless night in the cold, damp and dark cell.

The next morning, after a breakfast consisting of a slice of mouldy bread and a mug of dirty water, he was taken into court.

Here sat a stern-looking judge, with the king in a seat next to him.

To his surprise, Abu Sir saw his friend Abu Kir in the witness box.

His spirits rose immediately. "My good friend will certainly vouch for my innocence" he thought to himself. "I wonder if he knows what the charge can possibly be?"

"Abu Sir," the judge demanded sternly, "who sent you to murder our beloved king?"

He prepared the special cream Abu Kir had recommended, as a surprise for the king.

The king ordered Abu Sir to be arrested and two slaves rushed forward to grab the barber.

"Why, no-one!" Abu Sir gasped.

"How then do you plead?" asked the judge.

"Not guilty, of course" Abu Sir replied. "I am completely innocent."

"Let us hear the evidence of the witness, Abu Kir," the judge ordered.

Abu Kir stood up in the witness-box and began speaking.

"This miserable wretch—a thief I had to have beaten not long ago—planned to murder the king. When the king visited his hammam he tried to rub a cream containing yellow arsenic and quicklime in the king's skin. He said it would make the king's skin smooth and white but in fact it was a deadly poison that would have quickly killed the king!

"But it was you, Abu Kir, who suggested I gave the cream to the king!" protested Abu Sir.

Abu Kir laughed. "Is it likely, your honour, that I, the Royal Dyer, would do such a wicked thing? What would I have to gain?"

"No," said the judge. "Abu Sir is obviously not telling the truth. To save his own skin he will tell any kind of story—no matter how ridiculous it might be."

The king had listened in silence to all that had been said so far. Though normally he was a kind, gentle man, the idea of someone he had helped trying to kill him, and with such a horrible poison, had made him feel very angry indeed.

Suddenly he stood up in his seat.

"Stop the proceedings." he shouted. "I have heard enough to convince me that Abu Sir is guilty of this crime."

"Bring him along to the harbour, immediately," the king commanded. "There is a fitting punishment for him."

Poor Abu Sir was marched down to the harbour until the king stopped and spoke to a captain of one of the vessels.

"Captain," he said fiercely, "take this traitor and tie him in a sack filled with quicklime. Then throw him into the sea outside the windows of my palace, so that I can witness him drown and burn to death!"

"Yes, your Majesty," replied the Captain, "I shall take him in my rowing boat and await your signal from the window."

So they rowed away from the harbour, but to Abu Sir's surprise, he found that the captain was taking him to a small island.

It so happened that the captain had visited Abu Sir's hammam when

To Abu Sir's surprise, he found the captain taking him to a small island some distance away.

it had first opened. On explaining that he had no money with him, Abu Sir had allowed him to have a bath free, and the captain had always remembered this kindness, and been grateful to him ever since.

"I have not forgotten you, Abu Sir," he said, "and the kindness you showed me when I could not pay to bathe at your hammam. Now, I wish to return the favour. Tell me what crime you committed to make the king so angry."

Then Abu Sir explained how the evil dyer had tricked him through jealousy, and that he was innocent.

"Every man who is successful makes enemies, Abu Sir. But fear nothing. I shall leave you on this island until I can send you back to your country. You will be safe here. I shall now go and pretend to do as the king commanded me. He will never suspect the truth. Goodbye. I shall send help, and return in a few days. Wait for me here."

As the king signalled the captain with his hand, his magic ring fell in the sea.

When Abu Sir had kissed the captain's hand in gratitude, the kind sailor departed to carry out his plan. He took a large sack filled with quicklime and rowed until he came to the windows of the palace which looked out over the sea. There the King was waiting to see that his orders were carried out. The captain looked up to ask for the signal, and the king stretched out his arm, indicating with his finger that the captain should throw the sack into the water. The captain obeyed and the king was satisfied that Abu Sir was now certainly dead.

Unfortunately, however, the king moved his hand so quickly in order to give the signal that a beautiful gold ring which was more valuable to him than anything else he possessed, slipped off his finger and fell into the sea before he could catch it. No-one except the king knew that this was a magic ring, on which all his power and authority depended. When the king wore it, if any man threatened danger, he only had to point at him and a sudden ray of light would beam from the ring and strike the man dead on the spot. Naturally, when the king saw his ring fall into the sea, he could say nothing about it, in case the power of the magic ring should fall into someone else's hands. Therefore, he had to keep his precious secret to himself.

When the captain had done his duty, the king threw him a bag of gold. Feeling extremely pleased with himself at having tricked the king so

Abu Sir cast the net in the sea and when he drew it was full of fish.

skilfully and saved his friend, the captain rowed off.

Soon the news that Abu Sir had paid the price of his treachery and was dead became known throughout the city. Abu Kir, of course, was very pleased! He would not be troubled by his rival any more.

Abu Sir, meanwhile, had been left alone on the island, except for a fishing net that the captain had left him. The captain had told Abu Sir to catch as many fish as he could with it, and he would send some fishermen at the end of each day to collect all that he caught and take it back to the city. In order to take his mind off his loneliness and also to find something to eat, Abu Sir cast the net into the sea. When he drew it out again, it was so full of fish of every size, kind and colour, that he exclaimed to himself:

"Oh! It is such a long time since I have eaten fish. These will taste delicious. The captain said he would send some fishermen to the island to collect all the fish I had caught, as soon as it was safe to do so. I wonder when they will arrive? If they come soon, I shall get them to fry the fish in oil for me, and then we can eat them for supper!"

The barber's first catch was so large, however, that he picked out the biggest and best fish from the net, and took the great knife he always carried hidden under his belt. With it he slit open the fish, but when he drew out the blade—there was a gold ring hanging on the end! It was the ring that the careless king had let fall into the water, and the fish must have swallowed it! Abu Sir, of course, had no idea of the powers in the magic ring, and slipping it on his finger, thought no more about it.

Presently the fishermen arrived on the shore in a small boat, just as the captain had promised. The poor barber was so overjoyed to see them that he ran down to the beach to greet them excitedly.

"Here are the fish I have caught," Abu Sir cried to them as they stepped ashore. "I hope you have brought some large baskets with you to carry them in, for there are so many."

"Yes," they replied, and having filled the fish baskets, they started to carry them to their boat, which was anchored just off the shore.

"Tell us," the fishermen asked Abu Sir, "we had a message to come here and collect the fish. We could not find the captain however. Which way did he go?"

"He left in that direction, "Abu Sir answered, pointing with his right hand. He stretched his finger so quickly straight towards a dog that the fishermen had brought with them, that a ray of light immediately shot from the magic ring and killed the dog within seconds! It fell to the ground, dead.

When Abu Sir saw the dog lying dead on the sand, he started to tremble, and thought there must be an evil genie on the island! Terrified, the three

When Abu Sir stretched his finger towards the dog, a ray of light shot from the magic ring.

fishermen fled to their boat for cover, screaming with fright. Just at that moment, however, the captain rowed up to the island and Abu Sir ran to tell him what had just happened.

The captain explained that it was all due to the ring, whose secret he knew, and suggested they row back to the palace as quickly as possible.

Abu Sir explained to the king how the captain had saved him.

When the king learned of all the tricks the evil Abu Kir had played on the unsuspecting barber, he was convinced of the dyer's guilt!

"Throw Abu Kir into the sea in a sack of quicklime," he shouted. "The rascal must die! He is a rogue, a cheat and a liar, and deserves his fate!"

"But your majesty," Abu Sir begged on his knees, "please do not kill him! After all, he was my friend."

The King would not change his mind and so the wicked dyer was dragged away.

However, in spite of all Abu Sir's pleas, the king would not change his mind and the wicked dyer was dragged away to die.

"Now Abu Sir," the king said seriously, "I have done you a great injustice, and must now make up for my foolishness. All the gold and riches you desire are yours. Take them, and I beseech you, forgive me for making such a terrible mistake!"

Naturally, Abu Sir pardoned the king at once, and soon had more wealth than he would ever possibly need. However, he longed to see his home again, and so, one evening he bade the king farewell and with all his fortune, sailed off in his beautiful ship across the ocean.

Such was the fate of the evil dyer Abu Kir. The bay where he was drowned is known as the Bay of Abukir to this day.

Abu Sir, on the other hand, spent the rest of his days in Alexandria, where he lived the life of ease and contentment he had always dreamed of.

Maruf the Cobbler

Maruf the Cobbler

There was once a poor Cobbler named Maruf who lived in the city of Cairo. He was a very kind and honest man and had many friends. He earned his living by patching up old shoes and slippers that people brought to his small shop. His wife was named Fatima, and everyone hated her, for unlike Maruf, she was cruel and selfish. She shouted at the poor cobbler all day long, and was always complaining. Gradually, Maruf became frightened of her and trembled at the thought of her wicked temper. He even gave her all the money he earned to try to make her happy, but she always scolded him for not giving her enough. Although Fatima made Maruf's life miserable, he never once grew angry or complained.

One day, Fatima rushed into Maruf's shop and banged her fists on the table.

"Why have we no food in the house?" she snapped angrily.

Fatima rushed into Maruf's little shop screaming and banging her fists on the table.

"But I have so little money," Maruf stammered in terror, "that I cannot buy much."

"That is your fault! Get some cheese cakes covered in lots of honey. Don't forget!" she shouted as she went out banging the door in her fury.

But as no one came to Maruf's shop that day, he could only afford to buy some bread. What would his wife say?

"What!" cried Fatima when she saw the plate of bread. "Did I not tell you to buy me cheese cakes dripping with honey?"

Fatima flew into such a violent rage that she threw the plate of bread at him, and hit him such a blow on the mouth that blood began to pour over his beard. At this he lost his patience, and without thinking gave her a slap back!

"Help! Help! My wife is trying to kill me" he screamed as he ran out to hide in the mosque up the street.

Whilst he was praying there, in utter grief and despair, a Genie suddenly appeared to him, and asked why he was so upset.

In utter grief and despair Maruf went to the mosque to pray. To his surprise a Genie appeared to him.

"Alas!" cried Maruf in tears, "I am married to a dreadful woman who beats and shouts at me. What am I to do?"

"Do not worry, cobbler," answered the Genie. "I shall take you to Peking in China. There, if you are wise, you will be much happier and make your fortune. You have suffered the last from that terrible woman!"

No sooner had the Genie spoken these words than Maruf found himself sitting in a street in Peking! Whilst he blinked in amazement, a richly dressed merchant came up to him.

"Welcome, stranger, to Peking. I see from your clothes that you are Egyptian. Where do you live?" he asked.

"I am a cobbler from Cairo," Maruf replied and told him everything about his unhappy life with Fatima.

When the merchant learned that Maruf had not eaten a decent meal for two days, he took him back to his beautiful home and gave him food and wine to eat and drink.

"You need some new clothes, too," said the kind merchant, and soon Maruf was dressed in fine clothes.

"Let us go to the market where I shall lend you my beautiful shop" said the merchant. "You can pretend to be a wealthy foreign merchant. This way, you will get to know all the important people."

Maruf thanked his new friend and gratefully agreed.

So the next day they set off for the market, where Maruf posed as a wealthy foreign merchant, whilst his friend convinced

To his amazement Maruf found himself in Peking.

everyone he really was! When a beggar approached and Maruf gave him ten pieces of gold, instead of the usual few coppers, the other merchants were speechless with astonishment.

"What a rich man he must be!" they said.

In this way, Maruf's reputation spread throughout the city to such an extent that news of it even reached the ears of the Sultan, who called his Grand Vizier to him.

Maruf gave the beggar ten pieces of gold. The merchants were astonished at his generosity as they only gave a few coppers to beggars.

"Grand Vizier," he asked, "I have heard of a very rich merchant who has recently arrived in the city. They say he is from Cairo and is almost the richest man in the world! Have you seen him?"

"I have heard much about this man, your majesty," replied the Grand Vizier, "everyone is talking about him. He must have more money than anyone else in China, for yesterday he gave a poor beggar more money than most people earn in a month!"

"Did he, indeed!" exclaimed the Sultan. "I must meet such a man. Bring this merchant to me at once, that I may speak with him in private!" he ordered the Grand Vizier.

Straightaway the Vizier sent his guard for Maruf.

"Tell him," cried the Vizier, "that the mighty Sultan himself wishes to speak with him at the Palace!"

When the guard returned with Maruf, the Grand Vizier led him before the Sultan. Once in his presence, Maruf knelt down before him. The Sultan admired such fine manners and was impressed by Maruf's distinguished appearance. However, when he asked Maruf questions about his business and great fortune, all Maruf replied was:

"Your majesty will see when my merchandise arrives."

Since the Sultan was by nature a cautious man, he decided to

The Grand Vizier was ordered by the Sultan to bring before him the rich man from Cairo.

Maruf examined the Sultan's diamond and threw it on the floor. "I have far finer ones than this," said Maruf.

test Maruf and showed him a fine diamond.

"Do you have such fine stones in your merchandise?" he asked cunningly.

Imagine his surprise when Maruf examined it and threw it to the floor.

"But what are you doing?" cried the stupefied Sultan. "Do you not realise that diamond is worth a fortune?"

"Yes, but I have many far finer than that!"

The Sultan almost fainted with shock on hearing this. "I must have this rich man as my son-in-law!" he thought.

"Oh most distinguished Maruf, I am indeed honoured by your gracious visit to my city," he said. "To celebrate your arrival, will you accept my daughter in marriage? Together you shall reign over my kingdom when I die!"

"You do indeed honour me, your majesty," replied Maruf, "but had you not better wait until my goods arrive, for I do not have enough money with me to pay the expenses?"

Maruf told the Princess that he had no wealth for he knew she loved him and would help him. This she did, giving him gold and a magnificent horse.

"No! I shall pay the expenses of the marriage myself and you can repay me when your merchandise arrives!" declared the Sultan.

Maruf was shown into the garden where he met the Princess and talked to her all that afternoon. Maruf had not been so idyllically happy for a long time, and together they discussed their wedding plans.

The next day, Maruf and the Princess were married. It was the most magnificent wedding that had ever been held in Peking. Everyone was dressed in rich silks and brocades and sparkling jewels, the city was full of flowers and music, and the food was delicious. The greedy Sultan spent almost all his fortune to pay for such festivities, in the mistaken belief that Maruf would repay him.

The Sultan, however, was in for a shock.

"Your majesty," cried the Royal Treasurer running up to him, "I must inform you that we have no money left. You have spent it all to pay for the wedding, and now the treasury has run dry. The marvellous merchandise of your son-in-law has still not arrived."

"Maruf's merchandise is just a few days late. Be patient and do not worry, Treasurer!" the Sultan said.

The Vizier was very happy to hear this and immediately went to see the Princess.

"Tell your husband," warned the evil Vizier, "that his merchandise had better hurry up and arrive or the Sultan will have him executed for having deceived us all!"

When the Princess told Maruf this, he confessed the truth about everything, for he knew she loved him and would therefore help him.

"But they will kill you, Maruf!" she exclaimed. "Here take these fifty thousand pieces of gold and ride off. When you reach a safe place, send word to me so that I know all is well."

So Maruf disguised himself as a warrior and the Princess gave him the most magnificent horse in her father's stables. He quickly said goodbye to her and rode out of the city towards the mountains.

When the Sultan learned of Maruf's departure, he summoned his daughter and the Vizier.

"Why did Maruf ride away in the middle of the night so secretively, oh daughter?" he cried angrily. "The Vizier thinks he perhaps has no wealth and has tricked us."

"Father, how can you say such a thing! The Vizier is the one who is trying to trick you. Maruf has gone off to find out what has happened to his merchandise and hurry it up in order to repay you as soon as possible!"

"So, Grand Vizier," snapped the Sultan, "once more you have annoyed me! Another word of suspicion from you, and I shall cut off your head myself!"

Maruf, meanwhile, had ridden into the mountains and stopped by a waterfall to rest. As he was lying on the grass he noticed something in the ground a few yards in front of him. On examining it he discovered a large circular stone slab with an iron ring in the centre. Curious to find out more, he pulled the slab until it suddenly opened.

Inside he saw a flight of marble steps. He descended these and came to a huge cave, which was divided into four sections. The first was filled with gold coins, the second with pearls and rubies, the third with emeralds and diamonds, and the fourth contained only a small wooden box. This fascinated Maruf, and he eagerly looked inside. There he found a gold ring with a beautiful carved stone in its centre. As he placed it on his

Maruf rode into the mountains, where, as he was resting, he discovered a stone slab.

Being curious, Maruf pulled the ring in the stone slab which suddenly opened, revealing a flight of steps.

finger he happened to rub the stone.

"I am the voice and slave of the ring," said a voice suddenly, to Maruf's astonishment. "What is your command?"

"Could you carry me and all the treasure in this cave from here and put us outside Peking?"

Immediately after uttering these words Maruf found himself outside the city, sitting on a throne in a rich silk tent, with all the chests of gold and jewels ranged around him. A moment ago, there had been nothing there at all and a little boy who had been gathering berries stood staring at him, speechless with fright. He grew so terrified at what had happened that he ran home as fast as his legs could carry him.

The next thing to do was to take all this treasure back to the Sultan, so Maruf quickly summoned the slave of the ring once more.

"Now, slave of the ring," he said, "I need a thousand other mules, loaded with silks and precious fabrics."

Suddenly Maruf was sitting outside the city, watched by a little boy who had been gathering berries.

When these had appeared, Maruf set off towards the walls of Peking to take the anxious Sultan his long awaited merchandise.

Soon the procession of richly laden mules arrived at the Palace. The Sultan could not believe his eyes and ran to greet his dear son-in-law.

The Vizier, however, was furious.

He decided to make Maruf very drunk that evening when they would all be feasting and ask him the secret of his wealth. As Maruf was very tired after his exciting adventure, this was not too difficult, and when the evil Vizier had learned the secret of the ring, he quickly slipped it off Maruf's finger. He then rubbed the centre stone, chuckling to himself with wicked delight!

When the slave of the ring appeared, the Vizier shouted:

"Take the foolish Sultan and the son-in-law he so adores far away from here, to some desert!"

Immediately, then, the Sultan and poor Maruf were lifted up and carried across the sky until they were set down in the middle of a desert.

Then the cruel Grand Vizier decided to kidnap the Princess and take her away from the palace, so that if ever the Sultan and Maruf did manage to return, they should never be able to find her.

"How angry they will both be, the stupid fools!" he thought as he laughed to himself.

"How clever I have been! With this ring I can become rich and powerful!"

He rushed to the Princess's room, and having told her what he had done with the help of the ring, put it on a chair and tried to grab her.

"So you see, Princess, you have no choice but to come with me! Your

When Maruf's procession of richly laden mules arrived at the Palace the Sultan could not believe his eyes.

The Vizier slipped the ring off Maruf's finger, and ordered the slave of the ring to send Maruf far away.

father and beloved husband will die in the desert. If you will not come willingly, Princess, then I shall have no choice but to use force to make you obey me!"

"I love my father and my husband," the Princess cried, "and nothing you can do or say will make me go away with you."

"Don't be foolish, Princess," urged the Vizier.

"It is you who are the foolish one," snapped the Princess.

"Foolish or not, I'm the most powerful man in the world," shouted the Vizier. "Who can stop me taking what I want? You, weak girl?"

"You are only powerful because you own the ring," the Princess retorted. "Without it you are nothing, nothing, nothing!"

"Yes, I have the ring," sneered the Vizier, "and it's because I have the ring that I shall have you, protest as you may. Your beloved father and husband will never return, and there's nobody who will come to your rescue."

The Vizier went to seize the Princess,
but as he approached, she kicked and
hit him so hard he fell to the floor.

Saying this he went to seize her, but as he approached the Princess she kicked and hit him so hard that he fell onto the floor in stunned surprise. Whilst he lay there, she quickly picked up the ring and rubbed it.

"Throw this scoundrel into our lowest dungeon!" she said to the slave of the ring, "and return my dear father and Maruf to me, safe and well!"

At once the Vizier was whisked away like a piece of paper and flung into the deepest dungeon in all China! Within seconds the Sultan and Maruf appeared in the room, both deeply shocked at their brief adventure. The Princess was so delighted to see them that she ran to hug them both with tears streaming down her cheeks.

Whilst they ate and drank she told them about the wicked Vizier and his evil plan. They all rejoiced at their lucky escape.

After the Sultan died, Maruf and the Princess reigned together happily for many years, but always kept the ring beside them, in case it fell into the wrong hands again!

Maruf and the Princess reigned happily together for many years.

The Little Hunchback

Chan asked Li-Yen if he could go home with him and entertain him that evening with his songs.

There once lived in China a tailor named Li-Yen and his beautiful wife Mai-Sing. Their small house was built beside the river, just outside the city of Peking. One evening when they were both making their way home, a little hunchback named Chan came up to them. He was well-known in Peking, for he was one of the royal jesters at the Sultan's Court.

"Kind Sir," he said, "May I come home with you and entertain you both with my songs this evening?"

Li-Yen had heard of Chan, for he had grown famous in the city through the many comic songs he wrote to sing in the Palace.

"Why yes, Chan. I have heard you singing in the city and think you sing very well but my wife has not. So come home and have supper with us. Then you can sing and Mai-Sing can hear you."

Chan gratefully accepted this invitation, and the three of them started home.

When they reached the house, Mai-Sing quickly prepared the supper table on a mat of raffia. She placed before them an appetising dish of fish which she had been dressing.

Whilst they were eating, Chan suddenly cried out and clutched his throat. Li-Yen and his wife looked up in horror. The poor little hunchback in eating his meal, must have swallowed a small bone which had stuck in his throat and killed him on the spot! The tailor and his wife were both very alarmed. Perhaps they would be hanged for murder!

"What can we do, Li-Yen?" Mai-Sing asked in despair.

"Be calm, my dear, and do not panic. No-one saw him come home with us. We must quickly get rid of Chan's body and no-one will suspect a thing."

Just then Li-Yen remembered that there was a doctor living near their home, and decided what to do. He and Mai-Sing lifted poor Chan's body,

The poor hunchback must have swallowed a bone which killed him on the spot.

They placed him on the highest step and sped home as fast as they could.

and carried it to the doctor's house, a few streets away. They knocked loudly at the door at the bottom of a steep dark flight of steps which led to the private quarters where the doctor lived. They waited for a light to appear and soon one of the servants came down and opened the door.

"What is it you want at this time of night?" he asked.

"Please tell the doctor that we have brought him a patient who is very ill indeed. He must come down and see him immediately."

Then Li-Yen held out a large piece of gold.

"Give your master this gold coin as payment in advance."

The servant quickly ran upstairs to fetch his master.

While he was telling the doctor what had happened, the tailor and his wife hurriedly carried the body of the little hunchback up to the top of the stairs. They placed him on the highest step, just outside the door, and then sped home as fast as they could.

When they reached the house, they bolted the door and went to bed, praying that no-one had seen them.

In the meantime, the servant had told the doctor about the sick person at the bottom of the stairs. Pleased at having been paid in advance, the doctor quickly dressed and rushed out.

"Bring a light and follow me," he shouted to his servant. He was in such a hurry that he did not wait for the lamp. Unable to see, he tripped over the little hunchback and gave poor Chan such a blow with his foot that he kicked him right to the bottom step! The servant appeared with the lamp and they ran down to where Chan was lying. When the doctor saw

Through not waiting for the lamp, the doctor tripped over the body of the hunchback.

that the man who had rolled down the steps was dead, he raised his hands to heaven in grief and horror.

"Oh, what have I done!" he cried. "I have killed this poor sick man. Alas, they will throw me in jail and accuse me of murder. What can I do?"

The poor doctor was terrified, yet in spite of his fright, he took the precaution of closing the door so that no-one who was passing through the street would see the unfortunate accident. He took the body upstairs and carried it in to his home. His wife had woken up because of the noise and almost fainted with shock when she saw her husband carrying the hunchback's body.

"Alas," she cried. "What have you done?"

The doctor explained what had happened and they discussed ways of concealing the body that night, but the doctor could find no solution. His wife, however, was more cunning.

"Listen, I have an idea. Let us take the body further up the street and put it outside the Sultan's warehouse which our neighbour, the Moslem, looks after."

This they did under cover of night, and left Chan's body propped up against the street wall, so that he appeared to be asleep. Then they returned home.

Presently, the Moslem came home and was very surprised to see the hunchback asleep. Thinking he was a thief, he grabbed a stick and hit the poor little hunchback several times, until the body eventually fell over with its face to the ground. When he saw that the hunchback did not move

he examined him more closely. Realising he was dead, his rage turned to fear.

"Oh! What have I done? I will be arrested for murder! May Allah have mercy on me!" he cried, pale with fright.

Realising he must act quickly, he lifted Chan's body onto his shoulders, crept down the street and placed it against the wall of a furniture shop. Then he ran home as fast as his legs would carry him, and locked the door.

Just before dawn the merchant who owned the shop came walking up the street. He supplied the Sultan with all his furniture and was very rich. When he almost fell over the body he imagined he was being attacked by a robber, and hit the little hunchback with his fist.

"Thief! Thief!" he called out.

A guard who was walking in that part of the city came running up to the merchant, on hearing his shouts, and asked what was the matter.

"Guard! this thief tried to rob me," he explained.

"You have hit him hard

The Moslem was very surprised to see the hunchback propped up against the wall.

enough. Let him go!" replied the guard, lifting up Chan.

But when the guard saw that the little hunchback was dead, he grabbed the merchant by the arm and stopped him.

"Wait a minute! You have killed him! You must come with me to see the magistrate."

The poor merchant soon found himself in prison with plenty of time to think about what he had done and his probable fate. He could not understand, however, how only one blow could have killed poor Chan. He thought it very strange.

Since Chan was a royal jester, the magistrate had to seek the decision of the Sultan before he could sentence the poor merchant.

Having heard the story, the Sultan was so angry that he did not hesitate to answer.

"I have no mercy for anyone who is a murderer! Go, do your duty, magistrate, and see the villain is hanged!"

So the poor merchant in misery and despair prepared to die. He could do nothing to save himself.

The merchant imagined he was being attacked by a robber and hit the hunchback.

Two days later, he was led out into the market square to be hanged at the gallows. The executioner was just about to place the rope around the merchant's neck when the Moslem rushed into the square through the crowd.

"Stop! Stop!" he called out, "it was not the merchant who committed the murder, but I!"

The Moslem was seized and questioned by the magistrate. He gave him a detailed account of how he had accidentally killed the hunchback. Then he confessed to having removed the body to where the merchant had found it.

The magistrate had no choice but to release the astonished merchant from the gallows.

"Free the merchant!" he ordered, "and in his place hang this man who by his own confession is guilty!"

As the executioner was about to place the rope round the merchant's neck the Moslem rushed through the crowd.

The executioner immediately untied the merchant's hands and told him he was free to go.

In his place the Moslem now waited to die. But at that very moment the doctor ran into the square.

"Stop the execution before it is too late!" he shouted.

"Sir," he explained to the magistrate, "this Moslem is innocent. I am the guilty one. Last night two strangers, a man and a woman, knocked at my door saying they had brought a very sick man with them. I rushed out in the dark and fell over the body in my haste. Unfortunately, I kicked him so hard that he fell from the top of the stairs to the bottom. It was then that I discovered he was dead and that I had killed him! My wife and I were so afraid that we carried the body to the Sultan's warehouse which the Moslem looks after. We left the body leaning against the street wall, as if the boy were asleep. Obviously, the Moslem must have thought he was a thief and hit him. When he saw he was dead, he must have

In another moment the executioner would have hanged him if Li-Yen had not appeared.

thought he had killed him. Although it was an accident, Sir, I am the one responsible for the death of the little hunchback, and therefore you must hang me, not the Moslem!"

The magistrate was very impressed with such honesty from the doctor, and had to obey the law. As the doctor was undoubtedly the murderer, therefore, he ordered the guards to release the Moslem, and seize the new culprit. The executioner then placed the rope around the doctor's neck. In another moment he would have hanged him, if Li-Yen had not suddenly appeared.

"Sir, you have nearly hanged three innocent people. If you will be patient and listen to me you will learn how the poor little Chan really died, and that I am the guilty person."

The magistrate told Li-Yen to begin. He listened

carefully to the story of how Chan had agreed to have supper, became very ill after eating the fish, and died.

"I cannot understand what happened, sir" Li-Yen said to the magistrate. "A fish bone must have stuck in his throat and choked him. In spite of everything my wife and I could do to help him, he died within a few seconds. We were so shocked and alarmed at his death that, for fear of being caught, we carried the body to the doctor's door, and begged his servant to tell him to come down and see the sick man we had brought. We even paid him in advance. The moment he had gone upstairs to fetch the doctor, we carried the little hunchback to the top of the stairs, and laid him on the first step. When the doctor rushed out of the door, he would not have seen poor Chan lying there, and could not help falling over him and sending him flying down the stairs. So you see, Sir, it was all my fault, and the merchant, the Moslem and the doctor are innocent."

The magistrate was annoyed that he had been kept in the square so long whilst they found the real murderer. "Let the doctor go then, and hang the tailor Li-Yen, executioner!" he ordered. "This case has taken far too long."

Poor Li-Yeng was duly marched up to the executioner who prepared to place the rope around his neck. By now, because of the commotion in the square, a huge crowd had assembled.

"How unlucky I am to have to die for something which was an accident and therefore not really my fault!" thought Li-Yen, who felt sure his last moment had come.

Just as they were about to finally hang poor Li-Yen the Sultan's messenger suddenly ran into the square shouting and waving his arms in the air to attract the attention of the executioner and the magistrate before it was too late.

"Stop the execution! Do not hang that man!" he cried, much to Li-Yen's surprise. "I have an urgent message from the Sultan himself. He commands you, magistrate, to bring the prisoner and all the others concerned in this case to him at the palace without delay. He also wishes to see the little hunchback Chan's body."

The executioner hesitated and looked at the magistrate, who, raising his eyes to heaven, told him to free Li-Yen.

Poor Li-Yen was quickly untied and led from the gallows towards the palace and the great Sultan himself.

Why—you are no doubt asking yourself—had the Sultan suddenly stopped Li-Yen's execution and asked for the body of the little hunchback to be taken to his palace?

This is what had happened:

There was a very wise barber in Peking, a man greatly skilled in medical matters.

Before Li-Yen appeared in the square to stop the doctor's execution, this wise barber had joined the crowd there and was very curious to find out what all the fuss and noise was about. He asked someone in the crowd, and this man told him the whole story of how the hunchback had died.

As soon as he heard this, the barber rushed off to the Sultan's palace, where he demanded to be allowed to see the Sultan.

At first the guards thought they were dealing with a madman, and refused to let the barber enter.

The barber then insisted on seeing the captain of the guard.

"What business has a common barber with our great Sultan?" the captain asked him. "He already employs the finest barbers in the land. An old man like you has no chance at all of getting a job here!"

"Surely you would not want an innocent man to die?" the barber replied.

The barber begged the Sultan to allow him to examine the body of the little hunchback.

After a great deal of argument the barber was finally allowed to see the Sultan.

"Your majesty, please let me help you in this grave matter of the hunchback Chan" he asked.

The Sultan looked keenly at the old barber with his wrinkled face, white beard and the longest nose he had ever seen.

"But the man who killed my favourite jester is about to be hanged. How do you think you can be of assistance? What can you possibly do?"

"Are you quite sure that the hunchback is really dead?" the barber asked.

"Well, I haven't seen his body" replied the Sultan.

"Then, my lord, please let me examine the little hunchback closely," pleaded the barber. "And hold up the execution while I do so."

So it was that Li-Yen was taken from the scaffold to the Sultan's palace, and the body of the little hunchback was also taken there.

The barber looked at Chan carefully. Then he took a small box from a pocket inside his long green cloak and opened it. Inside the box was some ointment and a pair of pincers.

The barber rubbed some of the ointment on Chan's throat, while the Sultan, Li-Yen and all the members of the court looked on in silence.

Next, the barber bent over Chan and then held up the pincers for all to see. Gripped firmly in them was a small fish!

Almost immediately, the little hunchback sneezed and stood up on his feet. He was not dead at all!

A gasp of astonishment went up from everyone, including Li-Yen.

"No man dies without a cause," the barber said.

"Bravo, barber!" said the Sultan, bursting into laughter, and soon everyone was roaring with laughter, too.

Chan began singing and dancing round the room, and this made them laugh even more, so that soon all Peking could hear them.

What had impressed the Sultan was not so much seeing the little hunchback brought back to life again after having appeared dead for a night and almost a day—remarkable though this was—but the wonderful skill and cleverness of a humble barber.

*A small fish was gripped in the pincers—
the hunchback was not dead after all! Soon
everyone was laughing and Chan danced round the room.*

The Sultan was so delighted with the way things had turned out, and so filled with admiration for the wise barber, that he ordered the whole story of the little hunchback Chan to be straightaway written down in gold lettering on a parchment scroll. Such a wonderful story must never be forgotten, he said.

And this was not all. Li-Yen, the doctor, the Moslem and the merchant were all pardoned of course, but so that they would always remember the little hunchback's accident, and to make up for the fright they had suffered, he gave each of them a rich robe and a large bag of money.

As for the wise and clever barber, the Sultan showed his appreciation by granting him a large pension and the barber lived in comfort at the Sultan's court for the rest of his life.

Hassan the Ropemaker

Hassan the Ropemaker

One day in the Court of Baghdad, Caliph Haroun-al-Rashid was talking to a rich Merchant named Hassan.

'Hassan,' said the Caliph, 'I was passing your house yesterday and was struck by its extraordinary beauty. When I asked who owned it, I was told that you had built it yourself. I am curious to know how you managed to become so rich, and wondered if you would tell me, so that I might myself learn from what you say.'

After a few moments' thought, Hassan began to tell the Caliph his story.

'Firstly, my lord, I must start by speaking of two very good friends of mine in Baghdad, without whom I would still be poor.

'One is named Saadi and is very rich indeed. He believes that no man can be happy in this world unless he has so much money that he can live just as he pleases. The other friend is named Ali and has a very different opinion. He agrees that money is necessary, but believes that a man cannot really be happy unless he is good and honest and leads a virtuous life. He himself is not nearly as prosperous as Saadi, but he has enough money to live comfortably and be happy. However, although Saadi is far richer than Ali, this does not affect their relationship, and they are very good friends.

'One day they were walking through Baghdad discussing the matter.

' "I believe," said Saadi, "that the poor cannot change their position in life because they do not have sufficient money. I am sure that if a poor man was given a bag of gold he could use it wisely, and easily become as rich as me in a very short time."

'Ali did not agree with what Saadi had said.

' "I do not think the poor could become rich as easily as you say, Saadi. A poor man can become wealthy in many other ways, and often by accident he will become far richer than the bag of gold you mention would allow him to be."

' "I see that the only way I can convince you is by an experiment," said Saadi. "See that ropemaker over there, Ali. Well, I shall give him

Saadi gave the ropemaker a bag containing two hundred gold pieces.

a bag of gold. He is very poor and well suited to my experiment."

'So they both came up and spoke to me.

'"Ropemaker," Saadi said, "here is a bag containing two hundred pieces of gold. Make the best use of it you can, and see how rich you can become."

'"But, Sir," I replied, "I have a wife and five children and cannot, therefore, save or make much money. I work from morning till night and can scarcely earn enough to buy food for them all."

'"This is because you have never had enough money with which to try. Take it, and I shall be interested to see how you succeed," said Saadi.

'In this way, my lord, I was persuaded to accept his offer, and was so grateful to him for such an opportunity that I could hardly thank him.

'The first thing I did was to think of a safe hiding place. As poor people like me always hid any money we had in the folds of our turban, I hid most of it there. Then I went to the market and bought meat for supper.

'But as I was making my way home, holding the meat in my hand, an eagle swooped down on me and tried to snatch the meat out of my left hand! It grew so angry because I did not let go, it flew off with my turban and the money instead. I ran after it, but could not catch my turban. So in my misery I returned home sad and penniless once more, but with the joint of meat.

'Fortunately, I had put aside ten pieces of gold and I used some to buy a new turban. What would the kind man who had helped me say? A few days later, Saadi and Ali came back to see me and were furious when I told them my tragic story.

' "Hassan, what you say about the eagle is quite incredible. Are you trying to trick us?" said Saadi angrily.

' "Oh no, Sir," I insisted. "It

An eagle swooped down and snatched the turban in which the ropemaker had hidden his gold pieces.

The ropemaker's wife gave a beggar the clay jar in which were two hundred gold pieces.

is the truth, I swear to you."

'Happily, Ali had heard of similar stories of birds doing this in other parts of Baghdad, and spoke up on my behalf. Then Saadi made me another gift of money.

' "Here Hassan, take two hundred more pieces of gold and try again, but this time hide the coins in a safer place!"

'I immediately hurried home and hid the coins in the bottom of a clay jar under some corn. But after I had left, a beggar called at the house and my wife, not knowing about the coins, gave the jar to him for nothing!

'I cannot describe my despair when I learned of this loss, and told my wife about the coins.

' "Oh stupid woman," I cried. "You have ruined us just when we could have been so rich!"

'Meanwhile, Ali and Saadi though anxious to know what had become of me and the money I had been given, were longer in returning this time.

' "The more we delay, Ali," explained Saadi, "in going to see Hassan, the more wealthy he will

The ropemaker told Saadi and Ali how he lost the two hundred gold pieces in the clay pot.

have become and the more satisfaction we will feel."

' "I do not think this poor ropemaker will make any better use of the second lot of money!" said Ali.

' "But I have faith in him, Ali, and know he is an honest man. Let us go and see which of us is right."

'You can imagine their dismay, my lord, when they heard my story.

' "I believe you," said Saadi, "but you must realise that I need to be more cautious, since this little experiment has already cost me four hundred pieces of gold. You suggest something, Ali!"

' "Take this small piece of old lead," suggested Ali, holding it out to me in his hand as Saadi looked on doubtfully, "it will bring you a fortune."

'I thought he was joking, but he insisted, and left it with me.

'That evening, one of my friends, a fisherman, found that he needed a piece of lead to prepare his nets. As the shops were all shut, and I happened to have some, I gave him Ali's gift to me.

' "In return for your kindness, Hassan," he said, delighted with the piece of lead, "I promise you the biggest fish I catch tomorrow morning."

'The following day, therefore, the fisherman's wife brought me a large fat fish, as her husband had promised, so I took it home to my wife to cook for supper that evening.

' "Take this fish, my dear," I said to her. "Our neighbour gave me it in return for the piece of lead I let him have last night. It is, I believe, the only good thing that will come from Ali's old bit of lead, although he said

The fisherman's wife gave the ropemaker a large fat fish, as her husband had promised.

it would bring me a fortune."

'My wife was pleased with the fish and eagerly took it from me. As she was cleaning it she found a large diamond inside, which she thought was glass! Although she had heard of diamonds she had never seen or handled one, and therefore did not recognise its true value. As she was busy, she gave it to the youngest of our children to play with whilst she was getting supper ready.

'"Look Daddy," he asked me, "why does it shine so brightly?"

'I picked it up and gazed at it, marvelling at its beauty and the way it sparkled. At that time, I too had no idea it was a diamond, for being so poor we knew very little of such priceless stones. I gave it back to my son to play with, and thought of the delicious meal the fish would make.

'After supper, I was curious to know why the children were making such a din.

'"Daddy," they replied, "it is this piece of glass which shines most when we move it away from the light."

'"Bring it here so I can have a look at it and see for myself," I replied.

'When I saw how brilliant the glass became, I thought it was most strange indeed. What could the fish have swallowed? I never once imagined that it could be anything other than a piece of glass. However, as it shone best when the lamp was almost out, we turned down the lamp and placed the bit of glass by the fireplace. It gave off a beautiful light!

'"This must be the advantage that Ali meant when he gave me the bit of lead. It will help us save the expense of oil for the lamp."

'The children grew so excited playing with the glass that they began to shout and cheer. The whole city must have heard them.

'The house next door belonged to a rich jeweller and his wife, and their living-room was on the other side of the wall to ours. After I had gone off to work as usual, the jeweller's wife came over to complain about the terrible noise the children had made.

' "I am so sorry we disturbed you last night," my wife told her, "but you know what children are. Come in and I will show you the cause of their shouting."

'So my wife showed the piece of glass to her.

' "See, it was this piece of glass which made them so excited."

'Naturally, the jeweller's wife immediately recognised it as a very rare diamond, and gazed at it greedily. She realised that neither my wife nor I had any idea it was anything more than a piece of ordinary glass, and so she offered to buy it in her haste to possess it.

'The children, however, started to cry when they heard their mother talk of selling the piece of glass and begged her not to part with it. When I arrived home, I heard about the jeweller's wife, and decided to take the piece of glass to her husband to let him look at it.

'He, meanwhile, had learned from his wife of the beautiful diamond. Together, they decided to trick us into selling it for far less than its true value.

'After supper I took the piece of glass to show the jeweller, and straightaway he offered me twenty pieces of gold for it. Because I remained silent the jeweller, eager to persuade me to sell, suddenly shouted:

' "Come now, I will give you fifty pieces of gold!"

'As I saw he was so keen to buy it, I grew suspicious, and wondered why he wanted it so much.

' "That is far below the price at which I want to sell it," I replied cunningly.

' "Well then," the jeweller cried in desperation, "I will give you one

The ropemaker saw how brilliant the piece of glass became and thought it very strange indeed, but imagined it couldn't be anything but glass.

BAR.

hundred pieces of gold for it. Surely you cannot expect any more?"

' "Since this piece of glass seems to be so valuable, I shall be pleased to accept one hundred thousand pieces of gold for it, although I realise it is worth much more."

'At this the jeweller almost fainted with shock!

' "If you do not agree," I stated firmly, "I shall sell it to someone else!"

' "Finally I won, and the jeweller had to part with one hundred thousand pieces of gold to get the diamond he wanted so much.

'Suddenly I had become a very rich man. All that Ali had promised had eventually come true.

'The first thing I did was to build myself a magnificent house. Next, I set up my own rope-making business and employed all my friends, who were very happy to work for me. I bought warehouses and all the materials I needed. Now I own the largest rope-making business in Baghdad.

'Some time after all this had happened, my friends Saadi and Ali came to inquire what success I had had, if any, from the bit of lead Ali gave me. They went to the street where they had always seen me before, and were astonished not to see me there making my ropes. They asked an old man what had become of Hassan the rope-maker. Pointing to my beautiful house which rose above all the others, he replied,

' "Why, he has become a great

The ropemaker took the piece of glass to the jeweller who tried to trick him into selling it for far less than it was worth.

merchant in Baghdad and is very famous now. He is extremely rich and built himself that magnificent house which you can see over there. They say it is like a palace inside! To think he was penniless a short while ago!"

'My two friends were speechless with astonishment on hearing this, and naturally they decided to come in search of me at my house.

They arrived at my house and knocked at the door. One of my servants answered.

' "Is this the house of Hassan the Merchant? If so, may we see him?" Saadi asked. The servant bad them to enter.

'When they entered I recognised them both at once and I went up to them and greeted them warmly.

' "My dear friends," I cried, "I have not forgotten how poor I used to be and that I owe all the wealth I now possess to you both. Let me tell you how it all happened, and how lucky I have been! Even now, I can scarcely believe my good fortune."

'They listened in amazed silence as I told them the story of the lead and the diamond. I invited them to stay the night and feast with me and they gratefully accepted.

'The next day we rode to my house in the country. They

marvelled at the beauty of it and the magnificent position it had overlooking the river. They particularly loved the garden, with its orange and lemon trees, in which my two sons were playing. The eldest one suddenly grabbed something yellow from the branches and jumping to the ground, ran to join us inside.

'"Look father what I have found in a nest," he shouted excitedly.

'It was my turban, the one which the eagle had carried off. We were all astonished and when I showed Saadi and Ali the money still hidden in its folds, they saw that I had been telling the truth about losing the gold.

'We then rode back to Baghdad, and found there was no corn in the house for the horses. I sent one of my slaves to find some, and he returned with a jar of some that he had managed to find. When he emptied it out, there was the second sum of money I had lost!

'Thus Saadi and Ali saw that I had made my fortune honestly from the small piece of lead.

A most beautiful house and in a magnificent position overlooking the river. In the garden grew orange and lemon trees.

' "When you gave me the first bag of gold," I said to Saadi, "I was afraid that I should lose it, and didn't really know how to use it."

' "But you were honest, and told him the truth" said Ali. "Others would have run away."

' "It was the same when Saadi gave me the second bag of gold," I said. "My failing was that I didn't tell my wife, for I feared she would spend it foolishly."

' "But again you told the truth to Saadi," said Ali.

' "It was the only thing I could do," I replied. "Even so, I could hardly have blamed you had you thought that I intended to steal the money."

' "That is true," Ali remarked. "In fact, Saadi, I'm sure you thought that very thing. Is that not so, Saadi?"

' "Yes and no," Saadi replied. "Yes, I thought it was risky to give money to a poor ropemaker, and no, our friend had all the appearances of being honest."

' "You see I was right, Saadi," said Ali.

' "Yes, I admit it now," murmured Saadi.

' "The important lesson is that having money is by no means the only way to make one richer. In fact, money was of no use at all to our friend,

Hassan's son grabbed something yellow from the branches. It was the turban the eagle had seized and carried off.

Inquiring about Hassan's success, Saadi and Ali asked an old man what had become of the ropemaker.

for he lost it not once but twice. The great riches we see all about us came from the old piece of lead I gave him," explained Ali.

' "I shall always be grateful to you, Ali," I said from my heart. "My home and my wealth is always at your service."

' "That I know," answered Ali. "You see, Saadi, not only has our friend attained great wealth from my simple gift, but we have made a life-long friend. What could be more rewarding?"

'And it is true, Ali and Saadi are like one of my family, and my children look up to them as kind uncles.

'For my part, I have always followed Ali's belief that a man cannot really be happy unless he is good and honest and leads a truly virtuous life. Further, I have made sure that my children believe the same, for their happiness is very dear to me.'

The slave returned with a jar of corn. When he emptied it, there was the second sum!